HIS NAME ~ WAS ~ ELLIS

a novel

Joseph
Libonati

atmosphere press

Published by Atmosphere Press

Cover design by Josep Lledo

atmospherepress.com

For my greatest teachers—Joseph and Antoinette.
For my greatest love—Olivia.

In memory of Ellis and Joseph.

"The mass of men lead lives of quiet desperation."

- Henry David Thoreau

Prologue

The Boston Globe

Wednesday, September 6, 2006

Local Artist Institutionalized

BOSTON (AP) - Zach Foster, a local artist was admitted to Boston City Hospital for psychiatric evaluation earlier this week. Reportedly, Foster was displaying aggressive behavior during the Fenway anti-Iraq war rally before being apprehended by Boston Police. Foster gained notoriety for stirring up the national debate regarding the first amendment rights of artists after his controversial exhibition at the Museum of Fine Arts last spring.

~1~

Zach

I swerve to miss the silver BMW cuttin' into my lane. Boston's known for its shit drivers, but it gets wicked bad when the weather sucks. Even though I feel like smashin' into the son-of-a-bitch, I still hit the brakes. Cursin' under my breath, I try to chill like Pergo always tells me to do, but only after I flip-off the little prick. The douche turns his girlish, white-faced attention towards his dash and pretends to ignore my gesture. God forbid he act like a man.

Breathe, breathe, breathe, that's it...that's bettaa... until...

The jeep behind me's too close. Yeah, I see 'em in the rearview, two hipsters in purple Amherst sweatshirts. *Oh, here's a lesson fellaas...THOU SHALT NOT RIDE MY ASS.* I hit the brakes. They're not happy when they gotta veer off, almost slammin' into a double-parked car. *Ha, ha... poor hydroplanin' babies, maybe next time you'll respect my space*. Now I'm gettin' the finger. Shit, they need to learn to control themselves better. I guess they don't teach that stuff in college.

Tempaa, Tempaa, Tempaa...

I arrive at Pergo's after a few more intersections and a near incident with a Buick station wagon driven by an old chowderhead with a red and blue AAA sticker crookedly stuck on his rear bumper. After circlin' around for an open parkin' spot, I find one reserved for patients in the alley behind the office. Because I'm a little early for my appointment, I kill five minutes singin' *Pardon Me* with the radio while waitin' for the storm to stop pissin'. The windshield's sweaty with condensation, so I wipe it a few times to get a glimpse outside. I'm not sure why I bother though. All there is behind the steamy, pale fog is a green garbage dumpster filled with soggy brown boxes meltin' away in the storm.

I can't take bein' closed in anymore and decide to make a run for it when the radio goes to a commercial. Leapin' out of my Tacoma, I sprint for the door holdin' my umbrella like a relay baton. Even though I hate gettin' wet, I wasn't gonna fiddle with openin' that friggin' thing again. Bad choice, as I'm drenched when I reach the canopied entrance.

After ringin' out my hair, I enter the buildin' through a tall, oak door leadin' to a foyer with a sparkly crystal chandelier and open stairwell. A few steps later, I'm at his suite on the second floor—**The Delano Pergo Psychotherapy Group**. I slip into the reception area and hang my jacket and umbrella on a bronze, antique coat rack. There's a pock-faced burnout pretending not to notice me as I settle myself in. In turn, I pretend not to notice his uglier-than-shit face. On the opposite wall sits a skinny spaz of a kid, with swollen pink cheeks, low ears, and bushy geriatric-like eyebrows fitted for someone way beyond his years. He's wearin' dirty beige sweatpants with red stains across the crotch, hopefully, ketchup...but da F' knows. I bet Pergo has his junior associates see those losers. Anyway, I intentionally find a remote seat in the corner, incognito, and far away from 'em. I'm tucked away just to the left of the door and within an arm's reach of a table piled high with magazines. I grab a few and flip through the glossy pages while I wait.

Stick-thin, aairbrushed models with fake white teeth...faancy shoes...supaaficial douchebaags...people are moraans... they make me F...in' itch.

Just as the vortex starts ragin' inside, they call my name to go back. I flick the magazines to the center of the table with the knuckles of my three middle fingers and walk to his office down a tan hallway with recessed lightin'. Movin' slowly, I take advantage of a foot massage from the soft industrial carpet.

The progressive jazz background hummin' from the ceilin' speakers seems to get louder as I approach. Pergo and I make eye contact—me wrinkled and damp, him statuesque behind his huge, polished desk—crisp and ironed. He stands and offers a friendly handshake and I respond in kind. I've always thought it's a joke to gauge a guy by his handshake. I mean, is a greetin' supposed to be some sort of macho contest? Anyway, Pergo's shake is fittingly stern but not an attempt to overpower me. There's an intensity about him, I see it in his deeply-set, dark eyes.

The office is fancy yet comfortable. It's got a library

feel with dark rustic furniture, clocks, and various knickknacks. Bright abstracts are tastefully hung around the room. Every time I lower myself into one of his oversized leather chairs, I feel like havin' a martini and a cigar. Ya know, like a steakhouse.

"Hey, to all you guys out theaa. I gotta tell ya, even though I like Delano, I have sincere diffaaences wit' him. I know he respects my taalent as an aartist, but he also thinks my antisocial behaviaa is beyond 'normal limits' and is rooted in 'naarcissistic egocentricity.' I'll let ya in on a lil' secret...I think he benefits from our convaasations more than I do. Mostly, my reason for even goin' to therapy is to help him get a bettaa grip. I try to remind him of that whenevaa I can."

Anyway, after we exchange some small talk, he offers me a cup of spring water from his fancy cooler and asks, "How are you feeling?" He sits with his legs crossed, in a chair facing me, in the middle of the room. My response ain't measured, that is, since he told me in our earlier sessions to unload my feelings without pause. His advice...'Just say it as you do with your art.' For me, that means buildin' the topic, blockin' in the under colors, settin' the tone, the shadows—never calibratin' details until the end—if ya can ever find one.

I say in a blunt tone, "I feel anxious and unsettled."

"I sense that. Can you isolate where those feelings are rooted?"

"Yeah, I feel like the rain's done it." Delano perches his gold-rimmed glasses higher on his Grecian nose usin' his middle finger. He asks me to continue.

"The clouds suffocate me. They make me restless... make me itch." I wait for a response, but he doesn't offer anythin'. I keep goin'. "The propitious blistaa always wins. If I could only let it bleed...my waants, my futuaa, my God, they'd all dine with me."

"Interesting quote, is it yours?"

"Who else?"

He leans forward and scratches his brow with his thumb. "I don't understand the connection between the blister and God," he says.

"I can't stand these F...in' Evangelicals and their holiaa than thou attitude. All they do is preach their faalse, righteous piety. They're annoyin' like open sores...like swollen zits."

He squints his eyes. "Do you think that is rational?"

"If I was rational...I probably wouldn't be heaa." I snigger, "Would I?"

"OK. Continue...tell me more about what upsets you."

"You mean like all the jagoff drivaas 'round heaa?"

He smiles politely, like socialites do at cocktail parties. "There sure are a lot of those. But I mean, what bothers you so intensely about religion...about people believing in a power beyond themselves?"

"Come on, we've been through 'dis before. How many times do we have to talk about these delusional, biblical faairy tales? They're like when you bite into a slice of hot, cheesy pizza and burn the roof of your mouth. Can't wait for it to cool, then wham–it lasts for days, it blistaas, it itches. That's religion, ya think it's gonna saatisfy your hungaa, but all it leaves is an itchy scaab. I think the gold crucifixes they weaa make a nice fashion statement though." I smile back with a cocky grin while makin' a cross with my index fingers.

Pergo pauses, twists his lips, and wipes his forehead

with a white handkerchief monogrammed with the letters DDP, before repositionin' himself into a more upright posture. He makes a conservative grimace upon an exaggerated exhalation that lasts several seconds—ya know, the kind of breath ya do for a second wind. With a swipe of his left hand, he corrects a few tendrils of hair that had fallen out of place along his perfectly groomed salt and pepper scalp.

"OK, let's forget about the Bible. Do you find anything to relate to in other books?"

"Nah, not really. I used to read a lot when I was a kid, but I got sick of it. Books are like a TB test—they get undaa my skin." I slap my thigh and laugh loudly.

He smiles indulgingly before taking on a serious tone. "Why? Don't you think we can widen our horizons and improve our humanity by learning about how others view the world? Reading is one way to do that."

"Come on, readin' is a virus. Christ, just thinkin' about it makes me itch. The goddamned authaa uses the reader's brain as a host to multiply his own thoughts. Readin' doesn't bring me towaard humaanity, it repulses me." I pause and nervously touch my forehead. I search for a tool to scratch, but my fingernails are bitten too short. Some cuticles are raw with crusty edges of dried blood. Others are stained with paint.

Whaar can I spit? Waz he want me to read? Infinite Jest for chrissake...

Pergo doesn't say anythin'. He just waves his hand like a frickin' traffic cop for me to continue. I take the cue. "Why the powaa and control...why do writaas think they can inject prophecies into my head? Come on, literary microorganisms aren't reality; they're a form of brain-washin'...of mind control." I sip my water and wait for him to respond.

This time he does in a thick, baritone voice. "OK, let's suppose that you are correct. Let's suppose that writers want to influence thoughts. Would you at least agree that not all writers are malicious?"

"I don't know. I guess."

He loosens the knot of his blue silk tie clad with a pattern of small golden retrievers and speaks purposefully. "Some writers may want to do something positive for the world. Their words may steer thoughts...but perhaps with the intent to help people. Some books offer recipes for making delicious food; other books provide recipes for living a meaningful, peaceful life. Sharing one's perspectives through writing is not so different from two people just sharing their experiences. Books are conversations."

"Hell, I think that even authaas who write for good, as you put it, still wanna control their readaas. My thoughts are all I got. No one's got the right to entaa my head."

"I don't understand why this is such a problem for you. You still have filters on what you let in."

"Yeah, but if the message is strong enough, it passes through the filtaas and gets ya."

He writes something, looks up, and asks, "Has that happened in your life?"

"Look at me. I'm Harry Hallaa."

While he jots down another note, I shift around in my chair tryin' to pull my favorite blue and white flannel shirt lower over my clammy, faded jeans. I start to feel trapped in the leather cushion, so I stand and walk over to glance out the window. Splattered water droplets are slidin' down the pane, first hittin' individually, and then fusin' together like little rivers. There's an attraction between 'em, each drop flowin' into the collective. I continue, "When it rains, I feel...isolated. I feel like there's not a single person in the world who undaastands me. I don't feel like I'm paart of anythin'."

"Is being understood, or being part of something, important to you?"

"Yeah, I think so. My life seems so abnormal. I feel like I have nothin'...nothin' to shaare."

"Hold the self-deprecation. You share a big part of yourself with your art."

"Yeah, but that's not what I mean. I'm...I don't know... lonely. Everyone looks at me like I'm a freakshow. The othaas, they enjoy their jokes about the weirdo aartist. Nobody gives a shit about me. They're jus' waitin' for me to cut off my frickin' eaar."

The words seem to echo across the room for minutes before he responds in a supportive tone. "Come on, Zach. You don't have to be lonely. Don't you think you might start by opening your mind a little more, by better putting yourself out there...by trusting others?"

Although the rain stops and the clouds start to lift, the room still feels dark. "Nah," I retort in a muted voice. "I don't think I can. I don't feel like I can relate."

He pauses and leans back in his chair. His movements make a ruffling sound, like wind over dried leaves. "Do you feel that you may have intentionally chosen this path? You've told me many times that your isolation feeds your art."

"I don't know...it's jus' that..."

He politely cuts me off, now as a tenor. "You know, it

requires a conscious effort to be part of society. What attempts have you made? You need to move beyond making excuses and feeling sorry for yourself. You need to start taking steps toward making your life what you want it to be."

Excuses...WHAAT...?

My face feels flushed, and my heart is racin'. I lash back. "Oh, how profound. It's all so easy for you, isn't it, Delaano? You sit here in this aartificial place, with all your books, listenin' to my problems in your little silo. Your whole life is just so friggin' voyaaristic. Your techniques, your science...it's easy to be the exemplaa of wisdom when you're an Ivy Leagueaa, right? Do you get off on knowin' about things that torment me? Do you feel like you're on more stable ground when you watch me wobble? At least my shit is real...I don't need to read about it in some book." I start to pace.

There's nowhaa to go, but then again, theaa nevaa is.

I stop and clutch at my dank hair before softly mumblin', "I know what the mud feels like when I wade through the bog. I know what it's like to sink...like I can't survive anothaa second unless someone comes and graabs me from undaa the pits and lifts me outaa the quicksand. Have ya ever felt that way, Dr. Pergo, or do you just tell me what to do after you read about it? Don't ya think it's all so insincere...so unauthentic? Fuck, you should be aaskin' me for help."

The room is quiet. He makes sure I'm done before he speaks. His eyes are directed downward as he smooths out his left shirtsleeve with his right hand. His fingers are long and rough, and the maneuver sounds like sandpaper across the starchy fabric. He gets up and leans on his desk.

"Oh, so sorry to have angered you." His voice is slightly raised but still calm and steady. "Do you think you know all about me after just a few months of therapy?"

I give him a 'don't know' shoulder shrug. He ignores it and continues, "Have you ever entertained that maybe your way of thinking, which is fully under your control, has you trapped? Do you realize that other people can provide meaningful, profound lessons that can be of benefit? Maybe if you were more open...you would grow into a happier person." He slowly walks towards me. "Have you considered that we all share common fears, anxieties, hopes, and dreams? No, you probably haven't, because you can't seem to get beyond yourself. Your whole shtick is very solipsistic, and in your case, very concerning." He sips from his water cup and then crumbles it into a little paper orb within his fist, webbed with blue veins. He shoots the tiny ball at a wastebasket across the room where it banks off the wall into the container. He softens his stance and goes on, "Why have you so narrowly defined your existence? Are you not responsible for where you stand?" He returns to his desk and flicks a small cluster of dust from its shiny top with the side of his hand. In a decrescendo voice he adds, "Why not be more open? Hear what others have to say. Listen to their voices, read their words. Maybe if you could find some common threads with people, you would begin to realize that you're not all by yourself in this world. It's kind of simple, you know."

Pergo normally listens more and talks less, but today he surprises me with his response. Maybe he's right. A stillness falls over me and I swallow deeply. Goddamnit, my eyes start to well with tears. For a short time, the itch disappears.

He notices the power of his words and tells me that he thinks we covered enough ground for today. He walks me to the door and says, "We'll talk more on Wednesday. Work on the imagery. You can do this, Zach."

I respond in a muted voice, "Thanks. AAlright, see ya then."

My head is spinnin' when I get back to the reception area, where I'm sure to gaze downward to conceal my reddened eyes. I quickly grab my jacket and umbrella and slip out the door. By the time I get outside, a rainbow is usherin' in the first sunshine of the day. Even though I'm not supposed to, I leave my truck in the same spot, and walk toward the Starbucks by Newbury and Dartmouth. Once I get past the long wait in line, I take my Kona out to the front patio. I spend a lot of time in this place. Among the shallow valley of brownstone storefronts, I sometimes find a sense of calm here. Today I need that. It's goin' to take me a while to recover from my session.

After wipin' some moisture from a plastic chair, I sit next to a pretty blonde with a pixie haircut and petite fingers that nimbly dance across her cell keypad. Next to her is a guy with a puppy, a blue-gray Shar Pei, with a chubby, wrinkled face, barkin' at tiny birds nippin' at sidewalk crumbs left from the morning's parade of scones and muffins. Two middle-aged guys wearin' matchin' C's hoodies are holdin' hands in the corner while smilin' at the dog. Students are slowly strollin' along the street, wearin' vintage-chic clothing, some still with remnants of green in their hair from St. Patty's. Their calm, late mornin' saunter is counterbalanced by the Gestapo-like Boston Parkin' Authority ticketin' cars with run-out meters.

The sun grows bright, interspersed with sage-blue

clouds. Like theater lights, the rays warm my cheeks. As I sip my coffee, I glance across the street and admire the paintings hangin' in the window bay of the Copley Society of Art. It makes me think about my life and all that went wrong.

Places mold people—that's why I often feel disfigaaed.

~~~

Dan

Dan has not had a full night's sleep since the divorce. It is 3:30 AM and he restlessly crawls out of bed to initiate his insomniac ritual of urination followed by a trip to the refrigerator for a late-night snack. Tonight, he feels lucky to find a few slices of two-day-old pizza wrapped in aluminum foil. After peeling off the silver sheath and downing one of the cold triangles in several large bites, he rewraps the remaining slice for tomorrow. He washes down the chewy crust with a few sips of ice water and contemplates his sleeplessness while gazing outside through a small, oval window onto Beacon Street, always well-lit and heavily traveled, even in the middle of the night. After ruminating about Taylor—about how they spent every minute together until they didn't, about how they went from college sweethearts (their friends used to call them Barbie and Ken) to enemies, about how she so easily found love, and how he was standing there eating pizza—he acceptingly sets the half-empty glass on the counter before walking into the dining room.

Careful to not wake the downstairs neighbors by causing the loose and squeaky floorboards in his converted, turn-of-the-century brownstone apartment to
~~~

creak, he gingerly walks on the outside of his feet, transferring his weight toward the middle, as sort of a shock absorber. Still, the old boards amplify his every step, and he is sure the neighbors hear his insomnia as he sometimes does their lovemaking. High voltage streetlights illuminate the deep scratches strewn across the old hardwood floors. He finds the observation symbolic and starts to script a metaphor in his most recent journal, conveniently kept atop his table.

> *Scratches—symbols of strength. Their existence made against the grain of the wood, unapologetically carving their own life before transcending into the next plank, where again they make penetrable impressions of equal depth. Like wrinkles around your father's eyes, scratches tell stories of the past, they are real, they are true. But like all things, scratches are impermanent—like life, like relationships. They have a fragile side, given their very being depends upon the wood in which they are injuriously inscribed.*

Although he often finds journaling calming and sometimes helpful as a sleep aid, he's usually too drunk to make any meaningful entries. Even on a good day, Dan realizes he's no Hemingway, but there are times when a few words of interesting prose spill—no—trickle out of him. After thirty minutes of penning verses, he starts to get bored and attempts to fall back asleep on the couch to the near-muted sounds of the television. It's drafty in the apartment, and he wraps himself with the green and maroon afghan his mother had knit for him when he was in college.

The morning bustle reawakens him at 8:30 AM. Happy with being able to at least get a few hours of sleep, he gingerly crawls off the couch and stretches his stiffened back using cat-dog postures before laboring through a few push-ups and sit-ups. After three sets of ten, he's huffing and puffing in front of the hallway mirror where he studies his expanded chest and triceps. The exercises provide some energy, and he is excited to start the day. After showering and dressing, he heads out in his new pair of brown, Bragano Cole Haan Spectators, with two tassels on the hood. Strolling by some of the trendy coffee shops filled with yuppie caffeine junkies, he picks up a sesame seed bagel with a light coating of cream cheese, and instead of sitting, eats as he walks. Given that he is early for his scheduled eleven-thirty meeting, he ambles down an alternative side street, one foreign from his typical daily march. After all, new shoes deserve a new path. Eventually, he makes his way over to Newbury, where on this gorgeous spring day, he feels alive among the cherry blossoms and storefronts. There he surveys estate jewelry, restaurant menus, and men's designer suits before coming across an art gallery sponsoring a West Coast impressionist show. It looks inviting, so he decides to go in to peruse the paintings. He stuffs the last bits of bagel into his mouth before entering.

Once inside, he becomes entranced by a large, impressionistic oil of a mother holding her baby girl in a lush flower garden. It's done in soft yellows and light pinks and greens. The direction of brushstrokes and the thick layers of paint are captivating, leaving him with a surreal feeling of being part of the work. Now he imagines three characters on the canvas—the mother, the baby, and him.

The experience provides an illusion of warmth and comfort, a feeling of family. As he drifts further into the painting, he reflects on what could have been with Taylor. They both wanted children. Then a gentle voice, "May I help you?"

There she stands, a serene beauty with a projection of depth emanating from her large green eyes. Dan admires how she is poised downward in thought, without makeup, without pretense. She is of the earth. As he regains his wits, he shyly responds, "Ah...no, I was just admiring this painting," while coyly pulling his tan, tweed jacket over his shirtsleeves. The young woman gently grins, obviously seeing through his tortured charade and asks, "Do you like the work?" Her voice sounds distant, as if underwater. He admires the way the top of her nose crinkles as she smiles. She has white teeth with a mildquiver in her lips, the top being slightly fuller than the bottom. He answers with a hesitant, nuanced affirmation, "Yes...I...I think it's so powerful...it's beautiful."

"That one is my favorite too. Are you in the market to purchase something?"

"Not really, I just came in here to...to take a look." Dan is so taken with her that he grows tongue-tied. He feels the nervous energy growing in his psyche and deliberately ends the conversation by glancing at his watch and saying, "Thank you...I...I need to go...I...I'm late for a meeting."

"Wait. Before you do, I think you have something on your lip." She walks toward him, elevates on her toes, and points delicately with her petite index finger, almost touching his cheek. Uneasily, he wipes his mouth with the back of his hand and feels a small smear of cream cheese under his nose.

"Oh...thanks...it was a bagel...ah...anyway, excuse me."

She half-waves goodbye to his amusing awkwardness as he quickly trudges out of the gallery, red-faced and embarrassed.

~~~

Zach

After I got out of bed this mornin', I looked in the mirror after pissin' in the toilet. My face looked like an ice cream sundae for chrissakes, with dark eye circles meltin' into anemic cheeks—like chocolate sauce drippin' down white vanilla. I looked kinda ugly. I'm thinkin' I might need a new mirror.

After downin' a small glass of OJ, I lace up my sneakers and jog over to Pergo's. It's a nice day despite a strong easterly breeze that makes the run a little tougher. I'm tired when I get there and pause to catch my breath before enterin'. I take the stairs slowly, but still two at a time, to stretch out my legs. After settlin' in the waitin' area, which today is empty and quiet, I'm greeted by Anna, Pergo's twenty-somethin', redheaded receptionist. She extends her long neck around the welcome window in an ostrich-like fashion and says in a high-pitched tone, "Good morning, Mr. Foster."

"Hey, Annaa. Please, It's Zaach. I haven't seen ya in a while. Things good?"

"Yes, that's because I was on vacation. You look like you had a little work-out." She points to my sweaty shirt with her neon orange nails.

"Well, welcome baack then. Yeah, runnin' sometimes gets my geaas spinnin'." She smiles while buzzin' Pergo on the phone.
~~~

He comes out to greet me. "Please go on back, Zach. I'll be right with you."

"Will do. See ya lataa, Annaa."

A minute later, he enters. "So, how are you feeling?"

He reads me—top to bottom. Yeah, tryin' to get in...waz he thinkin'?

"I'm OK, I guess."

"You look a little disheveled."

"In what way?"

"Well, to start, your T-shirt is on backwards."

I look down. Huh, he's right. I smile and spin the damp fabric around my neck with a seamless maneuver. When it's in place, he says, "Please sit down, make yourself comfortable. OK, so how are things going...are you working on your imagery exercises? Looks like you did some physical exercise this morning." He points to the water cooler. "Thirsty?"

"Yeah, I ran ovaa heaa, and yes, I've been workin' on the imaagery too."

"Is it helping? Do you feel any calmer?" He hands me a cup.

Hesitantly, "Yeah, I guess so. But I gottaa say, even when I'm in the moment, people still bug me." I take a long sip.

Pergo leans forward. I notice a small shaving cut on his chin. In a calm tone, he asks, "Why? What do they do to annoy you?"

"They just don't think. They're just so stupid. They seem to believe...whatevaa they're told to believe. Like, if it's on the news...it's true. If ya ask me, we're just a country of moraans—people that can't think for themselves."

"Huh, that's funny. Sometimes I say the same things

myself." He seems easier than usual to talk with today.

"Well, at least we agree on that," I say.

"You'd be surprised. I agree with a lot of what you have shared with me."

Liaa. How could you agree...?

Pergo smooths out his pants, which are partially stuck to his quads. "Well, maybe we expect too much of others."

"I guess so. I mean, if it's too much to expect people to be able to think on their own, then I'm guilty."

"Why do you think people should act as you expect? I don't remember who said it, but there is a famous aphorism that goes something like 'expectations are nothing more than resentments that haven't yet occurred.' Is it possible that you are resentful?"

"Yeah. Maybe."

"Have you ever considered the root of that resentment? Maybe it stems from your childhood." I stay quiet. I don't like to talk about it. He knows that and shifts gears. "Let's talk about control, about letting go of the past, shall we?"

I ask, "Is that even possible?"

"I'm not sure, but let's give it a try. You start. What does control mean to you?"

I pause before tryin' to give him a well-thought out answaa. "Hmm. Well, as an aartist, I guess control is important...I mean, I'm always in control of my canvases. I paint the messages I want, and if I don't like 'em, I just throw 'em away. My paintings are what I want 'em to be, otherwise, they don't exist. I guess you could call that control."

"I would say so. Do you feel empowered by that?"

"I don't know. I've nevaa thought about it that way."

"Well, you must. I mean it's your creation. As you just stated, you paint the message you want to paint." He holds his hand towards me with his palm up, like he wants me to give him somethin'.

"Yeah, but I don't know if powaa or control makes me waant to paint. I just do it to feel more complete."

"What does that mean?"

"Well, ya know, like sometimes I feel somethin' is missin', so I get the brushes out. When I'm finished, anothaa hole is filled in."

"I see. That is well put. Has there ever been a time where you painted something that hasn't filled in a hole? I mean, you set out to tell a story in a painting, don't you? Sometimes, maybe the message gets lost and the story doesn't get told."

"Yeah, that happens a lot. Theaa are times wheaa I work on a subject and just miss. Then I try again and miss again. It gets depressin' ya know."

"I can't even imagine. What do you do when you feel that way?"

"I just stop. Sometimes, I don't pick up a brush for weeks."

"That seems..." We are interrupted by a knock at the door.

"Dr. Pergo, I'm so sorry to disturb you, but we have an emergency call."

"It's OK, Anna. Let's take a break for a few minutes, Zach. I'll be right back."

Pergo leaves the room. I got nothin' to do. So, I look around the office and start to daydream about the bullshit that brought me here in the first place. My mind wanders.

Iraq...the faalse justifications, the pain, the death. My

paintings were real, and I'd show 'em again. Yeah, the exhibition was controversial, but isn't that what aart's about?

I think through the show. Deliberately. In slow motion.

The president, George W. Bush, hangin' from a cross, with a look of salvation emanatin' from his strabismic eyes towards the heavens, maartyrdom his fate. His cryin' wife, at his feet, with orange teaars traveling down her devastated, white face. To his right, his mothaa, the laargest presence on the canvas; she's wearin' a blue outfit, showin' a coolness that merges into her gray haair, cerulean mixed with white, green, and red. In the background, his fathaa immaased in a crowd of men rollin' dice. While Georgie Boy glares off into the heavens, his mothaa looks away from her son and husband into a faarest of trees with deadened leaves colaared in red, white, and blue. Each leaf floats to the ground with surrealistic intent. Everyone knows they represent the lives of soldiaas, kids from the heaartland that believe in God, country, and family. One fallen leaf is painted black.

Then the paintin' of his security advisaa portrayed as Maary Maagdalene—provocatively dressed in torn gaarb, positioned on her knees in a submissive position. Standin' above her with his pants undone is DICK, the vice president. Her face is the focal point of the work, with glistenin' shades of white smeaared across her daark cheeks. Her empty eyes relive the rape as she gazes toward the viewaa with a patriotic staare. In the background, awaits anothaa political advisaa, the fat voyeaa. His red, pig-faced smile looks down at her. He's next in line.

The third canvas—a group of men at a long table. They're sittin' in positions from the Last Suppaa. Their faces aren't easily determined, but everyone knows who they are. Dressed in business suits, they're feastin' from a central pot percolatin' like a witches' brew, painted with the symbolism of the World Baank. As always, navy blue blazaas covaa their well-pressed white shirts. They all have tiny flag pins fastened to their lapels, except for one at the table who stands in the Judas position.

I recall how the curator and me chose the viewin' order of the next paintings.

A realistic series of small pieces showin' dead soldiaas, disfigaaed in twisted positions. They were placed next to works of daark-skinned children wanderin' through rubble, lookin' for their paarents. I tried to captaa their devaastation by emphasizin' their laarge, hollow eyes. Then, we placed the 10 by 12-foot mural of planes hittin' buildings and spillin' fire and terraa into crowded streets, followed by the even biggaa minimalistic canvas of an empty box inscribed with 'weapons of mass destruction' in lowaa case. At the exit, we hung a torn Amaaican flag.

While most left the exhibition saddened and silent, others were just simply angry at the crazy son-of-bitch artist who painted such garbage. I didn't fail to tell that story. Like I always say...paintin' is real.

Pergo comes back in.

"OK, sorry for the delay. So, where were we?"

"Umm...I was just thinking about the situation with my show."

"What part of the situation?"

"I don't know. All of it...a bunch of things. I don't think you'd understand."

Pergo pulls up one of his socks as he settles into his chair. In a slow and soft tone. "If I may...I'd like to tell you something personal..."

"Sure. You have to ask?"

"You see, when I was younger, I was very politically outspoken...protests, the whole thing. I know I may seem conservative now...but give me a try. Maybe I would understand more than you think."

Huh. Pergo just doesn't seem the type.

"OK. Well, I felt the pain I portrayed in my work. The exhibition was an honest depiction. We nevaa should have gone into Iraq. Now, when I look baack, I wasn't tryin to offend soldiaas or their families. I mean, I know a bunch of guys from Southie that served...I got no gripes with 'em."

Pergo shakes his head in an affirmative direction. "Go on."

"I was so happy when the MFA agreed to show the collection. I don't know if you remembaa, but the Globe billed it as 'shocking and sad, with a mastaaful command over subject and theme that paralleled Dalí.' I still can't believe they compaared me with him. That's the best thing anyone's ever said about me."

"Your work was very powerful. It touched people in very deep emotional places." Pergo pauses and collects his thoughts. "Would you do anything differently now?"

"Nah...not aartistically, but I guess I couldaa handled myself bettaa. I don't think it helped when I told 60 Minutes that I wished the White House would have been hit instead of the Pentaagon. I guess I acted out of proportion to the Iraq Waar, like I do with everythin' in my life. I can't help it. I hate the injustice of it all—the aaristocratic political fucks, they make me itch."

He listens and scribbles something in my file while I

bite at my fingernails.

"Do you think you were dangerous to people who supported the war? I mean, you were so vocal and resistant at the protests. It wasn't just the art, people were concerned about how you were acting."

Dangaarous? Pergo pisses me off sometimes.

"No, I wasn't dangerous. It's kind of a ridiculous question. Isn't it my first aamendment right to express my opposition to an inhumane waar? I mean we invaded a foreign country, a sovaaeign state. People, real people, were killed and maimed. For what...? Iraq had nothing to do with 9/11. Talk about control, da' hawks just waanted their oil."

"OK, justified or not, the question is about you. Why did you react so strongly to the war? It already happened. It was out of your control. There was nothing you could do about it."

"What about justice...what about freakin' justice...? And if I was dangerous, too baad. A price shouldaa been paid. People need to own up for when they hurt..." I don't finish my sentence.

Pergo seizes on my pause. "I understand...more than you could ever imagine." His eyes wander to the window where he gazes at the sky for a few seconds. "Let's circle back. I have asked you to contemplate certain triggers that set you off, right?" He does a roundabout motion with his hand.

"Yeah, I already told you that moraans set me off. People that don't think for themselves—like Amaaicans that supported the waar."

"Well, blind faith in institutions can, for sure, be a problem."

"That's what I'm sayin'."

"What I'm trying to get at is that I think you get annoyed when people attempt to control you, or even control others, for that matter. Perhaps, you don't like the power structure within society. Does that sound possible?"

"I don't know...when you say it that way...it kinda makes sense."

"You know philosophers like Schopenhauer thought that people act on will. A will to survive, to power, to control situations. There are volumes written about how power is the fundamental tenet that motivates behavior. When I try to understand you, I find your individual will very strong, and when someone else imposes power over you, or you observe an imposed will, even on a stranger, you rebel from the deepest core of your primal brain. I think resistance to external control might be a central trigger for you."

Yeah, yeah...whatevaa...

I feel like I need to stretch. So, I get outaa my chair and walk across the office to glance out the window. On my way, I brush against his side table and take notice of a picture on top—a beautiful girl in a red sweatshirt. She has a great tan and a contagious smile. On the opposite wall sits a bookcase stacked with plaques, textbooks, and some green ferns. Some small DaVinci-like sketches that look like flower vases are also irregularly interspersed along the shelves. Behind the desk hangs diplomas, certifications, and honors. His Ph.D. diploma is from Yale, but the year he graduated is difficult to make out because of the glare on the glass frame. I'm not sure, but it looks like somethin' from the '70s.

I go back to the side table and pick up the picture.

"She's gorgeous, who is she?"

Pergo half-smiles and replies in a subdued voice, "Oh just someone..." He stops short. I could tell the photo means a lot to him and that he doesn't want to discuss it. I set it back on the table. He becomes noticeably pensive.

I try to break the vibe with some small talk. "Hey, do you follow Big Papi? Talk about powaa. He's unbelievable."

"No...I lost interest in baseball a long time ago. Hitting a little white ball doesn't do much for me. I've always liked sports that have more action."

I agreeably nod. "Yeah, I see the baasketball trophies ovaa there."

He slowly regains his presence and gets back to business. In a solemn tone, "That was a long time ago. I don't think I could make it up and down the court anymore." He takes a deep breath. "Well, anyway...what do we have to do to help you keep your eye on the ball of not overreacting to your triggers?"

"I know I'm difficult. I've been tryin' to be more understandin' and nonjudgmental. It's just really haard. It seems every minute of every day, someone gets undaa my skin."

Almost in a whisper, "I understand that...people can be disappointing and hurtful. That's probably why you have tried to shut them out of your life. But that strategy can't work. You have to learn to not react to other people's transgressions. You are not responsible for what they do...only for yourself. As we have practiced, when something bothers you, realize it, and become present through deep breathing. Ask yourself why it's bothersome, try to understand it, and then let it go. The imagery exercise of having perceived transgressions floating away like a balloon toward the sky will help you do that. Changing out of reactive thinking requires a lot of conscious effort. Remember, lashing out at others will just end up hurting you more than…"

"I hear ya…I really do. Maybe I'll be normal someday."

He snickers. "Keep going. You are making fine progress. I'm very proud of you." He politely smiles and starts to rise from his chair.

"Thanks, Doc."

As I start to walk out of his office, "Hey…umm, Doc. Can I ask you a quick question?"

"Sure."

"Why did you decide to become a psychiaatrist?"

"I'm a psychotherapist, not a psychiatrist, Zach. But to answer your question, I think people often try to do what they need most in their own lives."

This guy's an F…in' enigmaa.

***

"Hey, to all you guys out theaa. OK, I finally made it outside…finally. I can't tell you how stiff he got after I asked him about that pictuaa. Shit—that chick must be somethin'. Anyway, now's a good time to pause so that you and I could talk. I mean talkin' to Pergo is one thing, but I need someone who can undaastand me. Just heaa me out, it'll only take a minute. I'm not sure if I should use my Boston accent or not. We'll see…probably a little anyway.

"So, the othaa day I went over to Cambridge Squaare. Instead of drivin', I caught a bus. When it arrived, I climbed up the giant steps, nodded at the drivaa, and deposited my faare. I shuffled to the back row and sat near the window. The damp, sticky vinyl reminded me of ridin' to high school. The only difference is I couldn't dress comfortably back in school. I used to have to weaa a shirt and tie, ya know, the dress code and everythin'.

"Anyway, after I got on, this chunky, baldin' woman followed behind me and sat too close in the next seat. Her chunkiness spilled into me and made me feel like the walls were closin' in. Plastered up against the cold window glass, the daamp smell of insulation mixed with the faint remnants of exhaust made me sick. I tried to take some deep breaths like Pergo always tells me to do, but it didn't work. My temples filled with beadin' perspiration, my heart was poundin', and I felt faint. I got off at the next stop.

"When I finally made it outside, I was hyperventilatin'. The air was thick and chokin', and I felt the difficulty of each breath across my solaa plexus. Behind me flowed the green and silvaa Charles Rivaa with the backdrop of the Boston skyline. I asked, 'Can ya take me with you?' Fuckin' stuck-up rivaa almost never gives ya a minute.

"It's just that...well, most of the time, I feel like...what's the point? You're born to some mothaa who has two choices...take care of ya or put ya up for adoption—that's if you don't get aborted. Then some guilty, moral types decide to find you a home, and when you're difficult, volley ya from fostaa parent to fostaa parent like a tennis ball. At each stop, your new family tells you how you're a gift from God, and how they love ya as if you were their own. You get used to hearin' it, but words aren't the same as actions.

"Then you turn into a teen and feel like you're not as good at things as the othaa kids. People look at you as if you're different. Soonaa or lataa you find your way, your thing—you develop yourself. For me it was draawin'. It seemed like a good idea at the time, 'cuz that's what made me unique. But then, the bettaa you get at your thing, the furthaa you drift into solitude. Some think creativity is freein', but I think it's just an excuse for maladjusted, unpopular types. Don't ya agree?

"Anyway, if we make it past that, we hit adulthood, ya know...people who are supposed to be able to take caare of themselves. But who can do it? I mean, look around, everyone's so fucked up. For example, there's this old guy who works at the grocery store next to my studio. He comes in from time to time and watches me paint because I remind him of his son. He's tall and fit, and even though he has the body of a young guy, he just seems shell-shocked. Every time we talk, he asks me the same questions ovaa and ovaa again. Although I feel sorry for him, I gotta tell ya, I can barely stand talkin' wit' him. I guess other people feel the same way, 'cause a few days ago, I saw him sittin' on a bench on Boylston talkin' to himself. Underneath the visaa of his tattaaed Vietnam Vets hat, I noticed his blank staare was worse than usual. He was just sittin' there whisperin' the Lord's Praayer. Waz he think, God's gonna respond? You gotta bettaa chance with the rivaa, you crazy fuck.

"Like I said, what's the point? You don't have'ta respond. I just wanted to fill ya in on how I'm feelin'...ya know, words as a medium."

~~~
~~~

Dan

After calming down from his embarrassment at the gallery, Dan makes it to his office a few minutes after eleven. It is stuffy within the small space, and he struggles to open a painted-shut window to freshen the stale air. His office is one of the smaller ones within the department, which doesn't bother him, given its quaint efficiency. Admittedly, he daydreams about the larger office at the end of the hallway, but realistically acknowledges the infeasibility of that space until he is promoted to full professor. The university manipulates space allotment as a ploy to motivate faculty. The more prolific one is, the more chairs and tables one has access to.

Organizing himself, he unpacks his briefcase and places a folder that contains some editorial notes for the book he is writing on his desk. Adherent to the stack of marked-up, white pages are blue and yellow reminders of edits he needs to make. As he scrolls through the pages and inventories his progress, he feels a small sense of accomplishment in capturing the core ideas behind his philosophical system. He is looking forward to the opinions of his graduate students at their scheduled eleven-thirty meeting, appreciating how their insights have helped the work progress so far.

Chelsea, Jason, and Noah arrive with the punctuality of a Swiss watch. "Hi, Professor," they echo in harmony.

"Hey guys, come in, please. Sit. Relax. Can I offer you something to drink? How are things going?"

As they settle in their chairs, "Pretty well," says Chelsea. "We're a little nervous about our logic exam later today though."

"That's for sure," reiterates Noah, who looks like a

long drip of water in his stretched-out blue sweater. He rolls up his sleeves as he takes his chair. "I would love a drink."

"I remember those days, nothing logical about logic class," offers Dan. "Try to relax. I'm sure you will all do fine." He hands Noah a soda.

"Thank you."

"Hey, I like your shoes," says Jason. "Are they new?"

"Yeah, I bought them at Filene's this weekend. Still breaking them in." Dan wiggles his foot.

"Cool. Also...Doc...we hope you are feeling a little better," offers Chelsea.

"Thanks for asking, the divorce has been tough, but...I am healing..." Dan pauses and changes the subject with a positive tone. "Anyway, I'm curious if you all had a chance to read some of the chapters I sent you. I want to present some of those ideas at my BU talk next week."

"Yes, we have," they say in chorus.

"Great, from the pages I sent you, let's start with potential stumbling blocks I should consider?"

Noah responds first, "Well, with all due respect, I am not sure I agree with the basic premise of your argument. I understand the part where humans are biophysical creatures, basically comprised of electromagnetic energy. I also understand that you are using the vessel as a model for the individual, a being filled with electromagnetic energy. But the transfer of that energy back-and-forth between people, or vessels, for that matter, seems too simplistic to be a core explanation behind human relationships."

Like a protective mother, Chelsea chimes in with an authoritative tone. "No, it's not. Don't you think that Doc has it exactly right in saying that a selfish person absorbs all of the energy from others. They suck it in from the room and don't give anything back. They're energy vampires."

"OK...but is that really a transfer of energy?" shoots back Noah. "Isn't being selfish just a survival instinct, anyway? The big fish eating the smaller fish—the circle of life. It's the part of energy transfer that keeps tripping me up. The chapter makes it seem like a selfish person is a magnet absorbing all of the electrons from others."

Dan continues jotting notes as he listens.

Chelsea, an amateur singer-songwriter says, "So, when I write a song, don't I offer up energy and inspire those who can relate to it? Doesn't that make me a giving person, or as Doc puts it, an 'offering vessel'?"

"Yeah, I agree with Chelsea," says Jason, "That giving is the flip-side to selfishness. The giver offers up the energy from their vessel, while the selfish simply absorb that energy and hold on to it. It's the same thing with authors, or any artist, for that matter. They donate their creative energy for others to absorb."

Noah gets up and walks to the bookshelf before again rolling up his sleeves. He straddles his chair when he returns to the table. "So, are you saying that I'm selfish when I listen to music or read? By your reasoning, my personal vessel gets bigger with those types of actions. I think that's ridiculous," he says.

"Well," interjects Dan, "From a metaphysical level, you can absorb creative energy and be inspired for a time, but that interval should be limited, and you should perhaps let the energy drift back out of your vessel into the shared realm—giving it back for others to benefit. Energy isn't ours to hold forever. I think it should just transfer through us like a vector." Dan is talking with his hands, making cupping gestures around his heart. He pulls out a page from the manuscript and underlines a paragraph with his yellow pencil. "That's the point I'm trying to make in this section. That's where I state that a balanced person would follow the simple equation: Energy(in) is equal to Energy(out). That means to be in equilibrium with nature, we should consume just enough energy for sustenance and give the rest back to the shared realm. If we bring in more energy than we liberate, our human vessel grows and becomes hotter. This self-inflated ego eventually causes the vessel to rupture, like an overinflated balloon. Meanwhile, if human vessels offer to much energy to others, it causes those offering vessels to get smaller and smaller. It's just about balance."

Noah pulls the page closer and reexamines it. He contemplates Dan's response while listening to the others talk about a paragraph on another page. Directing her attention toward Dan while pulling her red blouse higher over her cleavage, Chelsea utters, "I think your ideas also fit in well with the Stoics. We have control over how we process incoming and outgoing energy, but how others balance their energetics is out of our hands...so we shouldn't concern ourselves with it."

"Humans do hold weak electromagnetic fields," adds Jason with a boyish zeal.

"Yes, but there are no physical data to show humans absorb energy from others," replies Noah after he lifts his large head from its downward reading position. "Therefore, the basic premise is not true, at least from a physical sense."

"It's more of an analogy. What Doc is trying to say is that selfish people have taken too much energy from others, which builds up their self-ego and can ultimately cause them to break. Conversely, people who offer too much energy can grow deflated and lose themselves in the process, which ironically, can also cause them to break. It is just a model system of emotional health. The vessel is just a symbol," adds Jason.

"What about sick people, don't they require energy from the healthy to get well. Are they selfish?" asks Noah after taking a sip from his Fresca. The can is wet with condensation, and it fizzles when he brings it down from his narrow, chapped lips, circumscribed by a bushy, unkempt beard.

"It's a good question, Noah. You should take another look at *The Gay Science,*" says Dan. "Look, I know you would all appreciate some time to get your thoughts together before your exam. Let's stop there for now. I think I understand where I need to better clarify some of the text." Dan secures the pages with a big office-sized rubber band and places them back in his folder. He pats it with his hand like a proud papa.

"Thanks for considering our time, Doc. But before we go, we've wanted to ask you how you became so passionate about psychology and philosophy," says Chelsea. "You seem to really live the discipline."

"Yeah, just call me Jung."

"Ha, ha. No seriously, we are curious."

Dan sits back in his chair and crosses his arms. "Really, do you really want to hear...I mean, it's not much of a story. My life has been...some may say...boring."

"We do. We don't feel like we know that side of you," she says.

"I'm sure you will be disappointed."

They laugh in unison. "Come on...don't be so secretive," says Jason.

"Well, I'll give you the short version before you have to go to class. When I was a kid, I played a lot of hoops. I was pretty good until games were close, where under the pressure of winning and losing, I often folded. I started reading this book—*Zen in the Art of Archery*, which was written by a German philosopher. It basically instructed the reader to become one with the motor task—trust yourself and your unconscious mind sort of thing. I found it fascinating and started to meditate before games. By the time I got to college, I was better at controlling my emotions, and I improved as a player. So, I guess improving sports performance was my first step toward this field."

Chelsea follows, "That's so interesting. Books really can change a person's life."

"Yeah, that's for sure. Then, there was my father. Even though he never went to college, he was always interested in the arts and religion. He loved books like the *Divine Comedy*. Somewhere along the way, he also inspired me to start thinking about things at a deeper level. That's when I got into religious philosophy. Now that I think about it, my dad also played a big part in me getting into psychology. He developed terrible dementia when I was in college. It was such a dark time. God, the mind is such a complicated force."

"Is your dad still around?" asks Jason.

"No, he died right before I finished my undergraduate studies. It still makes me sad...he would have been so proud to see that I'm now a professor." Things get quiet around the table. Dan rubs the bottom of his cleanly shaven chin. "Huh, now you have me thinking, there was also this event when I was in sixth grade. This kid from my class and his entire family were murdered by these arsonists...it was Valentine's Day...it was very strange, they were all found in a corner of their charred living room, huddled together...the mother holding her infant. I could never understand, or process...how people could murder...especially an innocent family." Noah and Chelsea shake their heads in disgust. "I think that event also unconsciously got me interested in psychology."

Jason asks, "Did they ever catch them...the arsonists?"

After a pregnant pause, "Yeah, they got them. If there's a hell, I hope they're burning in it." Dan's face turns a maroon red. "You know the irony? Even at age twelve, I wanted to hurt...no—I wanted to kill those guys. There were three of them. I mean, I was just a kid, but I had a burning desire for revenge...no pun intended."

Dan's comment catches Noah's attention. "I think that's completely understandable, Professor. They hurt a friend of yours. You needed to see justice...an eye for an eye. Maybe some vessels just need to be destroyed, you know, the violent ones. They are not just sucking energy from others, they are sending huge toxic clouds to squash others."

"Thanks, Noah. You may be right about that. But either way, I don't think it was such a healthy response. Especially for a kid. Sometimes I worry about my darker self. You know, even with all this take the high road vessel advice, it's easy to lose perspective. I constantly have internal battles to overcome my instincts."

"That's what makes you such a great professor," says

Jason. "You are a real person with real flaws. You show that authenticity in the classroom."

"Ha, ha. I'm not sure that was a compliment," says Dan.

Jason grins. "You know it was."

"Well, thank you. Anyway guys, I appreciate your thoughts and time. Like always, you have helped me see where my model is still underdeveloped. I don't want to hold you back; go get ready for that test. Good luck."

"OK. Let us know when it's time to review the next sections," says Jason.

"And Doc, don't forget I'm playing in Davis Square next month. Come check it out."

"Will do, Chelsea. See you all soon." With that, they shuffle out.

The conversation unearths some painful memories for Dan. He sits at his desk and reflects on his father's dementia. He knows a little about the genetics of the disease and is aware that apples don't fall far from the tree. He also worries about other aspects of his mental health, particularly his temper. He thinks about how his own behavior contributed to his divorce.

After deciding a walk might improve his mood, he opts to visit the library. He does a mile around the periphery of campus before cutting to the grand entrance under the large oaks that line the quad. After he checks in, he finds an open, quiet study space under a gothic-style archway toward the back of the eastern wing. There he reads a few pages about accepting change from one of his favorite Alan Watts' books.

Normally, Dan loves to read and ponder, but today he is having difficulty concentrating. His mind is darting all over the map. Beyond reflecting on his father, his boyhood, and his divorce—every time he starts a new paragraph, SHE enters his mind—HER eyes, HER lips. After an hour of not retaining much of anything, he decides to call it quits and return home to get his head together. He packs his book and papers into his briefcase, and slowly treks towards the Back Bay, where it occurs to him while crossing the Mass Ave Bridge to return to the gallery. Maybe she's still there, he thinks. Perhaps, he could make a better impression...cream cheese for God's sake. He reminisces on how confident he was when he first met Taylor. How excited Taylor was when they were finally introduced on the library steps. How Taylor grew so nervous when she saw him that she dropped her calculus book in a puddle. How he diligently retrieved it and wiped it dry with the bottom of his stretched-out, gray Champion sweatshirt. How the pizza they shared the following night, after the game he hit a fade-away winner from the right corner, with no time on the clock, led to something magical. That's the guy he was. He needed to find that guy now.

A few blocks later, he enters the gallery with a confident stride, paying little attention to the art, while directly casing the space for HER. An older man, busy meticulously setting a table for a wine and cheese reception, periodically scrutinizes him from the corner of his eye. A few gray-haired women who are admiring a series of small pastels on the far wall are in a deep discussion over their significance as a medium. SHE is nowhere to be found.

Dan nonchalantly looks around the store pretending to be interested in a table of Mexican pottery while hoping

SHE is just on a break.

Like a hawk on a hunt, the old man moseys over with a slow, deliberate gait. He is wearing a blue and green-checkered sweater vest and smells like candle wax.

"Good day. Can I help you?"

"No, thank you," replies Dan. "I'm just looking around."

In a suspicious tone, "All right. Please enjoy the art and let me know if anything catches your eye. You don't look familiar, have you visited our gallery before?"

"Yes, I have. Very recently, in fact. You have a lot of beautiful things here."

"Thank you, we do in fact. The grand painting near the entrance is from one of our more established California artists. He's exciting, isn't he?"

"He sure is. I admired it the last time I was in."

"The artist is the father of one of my employees. She's a wonderful young woman...Chiara."

"That's such a beautiful name."

"Yes...it is. It means 'light' in Italian." The man smiles. "Well, let me tend to my table. Please do let me know if I can be of any further assistance."

Dan reaches for the old man's hand and shakes it with vigor. "Sir, you have no idea how much you have already assisted me. Thank you."

The old man looks confused. "You are quite welcome."

When the man returns to the escritoire, Dan half-interestedly scans a series of classical landscapes, still hoping for HER return. After ten long minutes, he resigns himself to not seeing HER before hesitantly making his way to the door.

"Thanks again."

"You are welcome, young man. Visit us again sometime."

"Will do."

Dan walks out of the gallery, down four red brick steps to the crowded sidewalk. At the bottom, he turns to garner another glimpse of the building. He murmurs Chiara all the way home.

~~~

Zach

It's a beautiful day outside, so I decide to take a slow walk over to Pergo's office. The sun is large and bright, casting stretched, blue shadows over the Christian Science Plaza. A cool breeze tickles my face. It makes me feel calm and tranquil, a sensation that gets ruined when I walk past a group of Berklee students smokin' cigarettes on the sidewalk outside one of their classroom buildings. Their collective stink leaves a disgustin' aura around their sickly figures—hunched shoulders, purple fingers, pale lips. I see 'em but wish I hadn't. They gnaw at me, but I don't say anything to 'em. *F....in' Mass Ave douchebags.*

A few minutes later, I'm at his buildin' and march up the stairs. I'm right on time and go back to meet him without havin' to wait. He's standin' outside his office door and isn't even wearin' a tie. He seems relaxed.

"Hi, Zach."

"Hey, Doc."

"You look energized today. How's everything going?"

"It's good. I hope you're not gonna ask me about my imaagery exercises though. I have to say, they're gettin' a lil' borin'."
~~~

He chuckles. “No, we can discuss that next time. So, tell me, what have you been up to?” He points at the chair for me to sit. I sink into it and feel reflective, rubbin’ my hands together.

“Well for startaas, I have been practicin’ the imaagery... and yeah, I do feel bettaa.”

“Well, that’s good to hear. Keep up the good work. I heard you saw Dr. Swanson earlier this week. How did that go?”

“Good. She’s really nice to talk to.”

“Yes, she is. A wonderful psychiatrist too.”

“I guess.”

“What did you discuss with her?”

I hesitate before offerin’, “It was a little strange. She aasked me if I ever thought about suicide.” I squirm around my chair.

“Well, that’s a pretty big issue.” Pergo leans forward.

“I guess. At first, I told her no. Then after she kept askin’, I told ‘er the truth...that I’d thought about it a couplaa times. I mean doesn’t everybody?”

“I think most people do consider it periodically throughout their lives.” Pergo starts tappin’ his foot on the floor.

“Dr. Swanson told me to call her, or you, when I have those kinda thoughts.”

“That’s the important part. It’s crucial to talk to someone when you get into those dangerous mental patterns.” He pulls his chair closer.

I ask, “Have you?”

“Have I what?”

“You know...have you ever thought about doin’ it?”

He leans back and crosses his arms. “As I said, I think

almost everyone has."

"What has kept you from...ya know?"

He takes his glasses off and sets them on his lap. Softly, "Well, I don't think it's appropriate to have this conversation center on me." His face reddens, and he redirects his eyes to the door before continuing in a deep, almost rehearsed tone. "As we have discussed, I think this is where we must feel connected to people and find purpose in our lives. For example, I find my own purpose in helping people find theirs. Don't you think that you do the same with painting? You cause people to reflect, to have them realize essential elements within themselves... to find perspective."

"I don't know...maybe with some of my introspective stuff. But, I mean, don't ya think people sometimes get even saddaa when they get introspective?"

"Yes, definitely." He rubs his temples and puts his glasses back on. He says, "Introspection is like pulling the layers of your onion back. Once you get down to the core, you are forced to encounter your deepest being."

"That's right on, Doc. Peelin' onions and introspection can both leave you in teaas...Ha, ha."

"Huh, yes they can." He briefly laughs. "The trick, as hard as it may be, is to try to find one's deepest being in the exercise. I think without purpose, we can all easily fall into nihilistic malaise and think of actions like suicide."

"You're not gonna give me a sermon about how God gave us purpose, are ya?"

"That's not what I'm saying. I think people are constantly establishing why they are alive and the significance of that life. Isn't that just human? When we are striving toward something, our goal or purpose drives us through thoughts of insignificance. I don't think it is necessarily contingent on religious beliefs. It's internal." He pauses and twists his mouth. "I know life can be hard. You know we are always here for you if you start feeling that way."

I nod. "Thanks, Doc. I know you are." He writes a few notes before looking up at me.

"So, what else did Dr. Swanson say?"

"She asked how we're gettin' along in our sessions. She made a couple of adjustments to my medicines too."

"Yes, she sent me a note that she lowered your Zoloft."

"Yeah, she did. I told her that I thought workin' with you was helpin' me too."

"Good. Good. You are making fine progress. Just keep elevating your thinking. So, how about the art front... how's painting going?"

"Great. I've been in the studio a lot the last few days. I started a new series of nudes this week."

"Interesting, have you done nudes in the past?"

"Not many, but I'm really gettin' into 'em now. They're much toughaa than other topics. People don't realize."

"In what way?"

"Well, you gotta show somethin' significant about the person. Somethin' deepaa...gotta get undaa the skin."

"Fascinating. That profound level of expression is so important, isn't it?

"Yeah, I think it is."

"Are you using photos or live models?"

"A little of both. I met a few dancaas down on Waashington Street who are willin' to sit for me. The in-person stuff is jus' more real."

"The Combat Zone? I didn't know you go over there."

"Yeah, I like goin' down around six for haappy hour. You interested?"

"No, I think I'll pass. Let's talk more about this. I'm curious."

Sarcastically, "OK, sure. You need some girl advice?"

Pergo ignores me, before sayin', "No, but I'd like to learn about your relationships with these girls." He fiddles with the buttons on his shirt.

"No relationships heaa. I haven't had a girlfriend for a long time."

"I realize that, but harboring friendly relationships with these girls still counts, right? I mean the fact that they feel comfortable to sit for you is important. They must feel safe with you."

"Well, I think it's just flatterin' for them to know that I want to paint 'em. I think it makes 'em feel pretty."

"Well, aren't they?" He makes an open-palmed gesture.

"For sure. But they don't always think of themselves that way. These girls have real problems."

"I'm finding this side of you very curious, Zach. It seems like progress for you in opening up. I just worry that this type of environment may not be..."

I cut him off. "Come on. Don't be so judgmental."

"I understand the culture. I wasn't born yesterday. I'm trying to understand what you get out of it."

While pushin' my hair outta my eyes, "I like to watch the girls...look at their bodies. Why else?"

"You could do that in other ways, like videos or something. Can't you paint from a photo? I think it's more than that. There's something more significant motivating you."

"Well, it's different in person. I like talkin' with 'em too...gettin' to know 'em."

"What do you talk about?"

"Mostly, we talk about their problems. I've even turned 'em on to some of the imaagery techniques that you taught me. Anyway, most of the time, we have honest discussions."

"What do you mean?"

"Well, these girls aren't out to impress anyone. They just tell me about their broken lives. Bunches of 'em have been molested or on drugs...you know, now they have to dance to take care of their haabits. A couple even have kids. Some of 'em like to ask my advice on their boyfriends and stuff."

"Do you give them advice?"

"Well, I tell 'em what I think."

"In what way?"

You're gettin' on my nerves with these questions. I take a deep breath and respond as calmly as I can. "I don't know. What kind of question is that? I mean they ask me about stuff, and I give 'em my opinions. For exaample, this one girl asked me if I thought she should go to Vegaas to dance at a biggaa venue. You should see 'er, a tall Russian...long legs. I told her that she'd be crazy not to, that she has real beauty and taalent. She took my advice and made it big. One night I caught her on Stern. Shit, she moved to LA and staarred in a bunch of B movies."

Pergo pauses. I can tell he's not happy with me not mentioning this to him earlier. I guess he thinks my counseling is nothing more than the blind leading the blind. "Zach...when these girls ask you for your advice, does that make you feel important?"

"Yeah, I suppose." I straighten in my chair.

"Would you say it may even make you feel powerful, like there are people who are even more fragile than you are?"

"God, I don't know why you have to ovaanalyze everythin'. That's why I haven't mentioned this before. Can't we change the topic?"

"No, I'm not going to let you off the hook on this. What do you get out of it...is it really talking? Maybe you do it for sex."

"No, there's no sex. OK, sometimes they let me grab their tits...but...I mean, that's not why. I just like being theaa. I like 'em. I like to paint them." I pause for a few seconds. Pergo lets me stew. "Sometimes it's the only place that makes me feel alive."

"What does alive mean?" His glasses are hanging low on his nose. He takes them off, blows a moist breath over 'em, and wipes 'em with his hanky. I watch him do his ritual before lookin' over his shoulder at the abstract paintings near his desk.

"Like, every day, I'm doin' this imagery bullshit, or paintin', or walkin' around town. I'm jus' bored with it all. Christ, nothin' seems to stimulate me. Yeah, I find the girls sexy, but that's not why I go. I feel alive when I'm around 'em. They give me energy. They make me want to create."

"Do they make you feel significant? Maybe they cater to you because you're tipping them?"

"Fuck, Delano. I don't caare why. Do you know how alone I feel? If they distract me from myself for a few hours, then I just don't give a shit. What's the problem?"

We both look intently at one another. Softly, he says, "It's a big problem. You need to learn how to live well in your own head...not relative to others who need help."

"You know, you spend a lot of time judgin' me."

"I'm not judging you. I'm trying to help you. Do you really think that by feeding your ego, these girls are benefiting you? You need to do exactly the opposite. You need to stop feeding the self. We have talked about this. Your ego is the problem—it has you separated from the rest of the world."

"OK, Sigmund. But you told me to put myself out theaa."

"You can be smart all you want, but you know what I meant. Put yourself out there in the real world, with real people, that you don't have to pay to gain attention. While you are certainly doing better, this kind of thing is holding your progress back. Believe me, I've been through similar challenges in my own life."

"I doubt it. You seem like you were born perfect."

"If you only knew, Zach...if you only knew."

~~~

Dan

Dan arrives at BU thirty minutes before his talk. He is greeted by his old grad school friend and colleague, Paolo Bettullio. Paolo joined the BU faculty after a short academic stint at Tufts and was now Chair of Philosophy. Dan and Paolo had kept in touch through the years, regularly meeting for dinners or a glass of wine. However, since his split with Taylor, Dan and Paolo didn't get together so frequently. Dan thought Paolo might be avoiding him because he was uncomfortable with the topic of divorce. Paolo believed in the simplicity of family. He and his wife, Francesca, lived in an elegantly furnished
~~~

apartment in the North End. They were often admired strolling together down Hanover, stopping in gelato and pastry shops, wonderfully in love. While Dan envied their dedication to one another, he felt abandoned by them since he and Taylor split. That was until Paolo invited him to present his newest paradigm to the graduate program.

Paolo, a burly man with an even larger personality, cordially greets Dan with an excited, robust hug. "Ciao, Dan. You ahh look great!"

"You too, Paolo. It's so nice to see you. You have become such a clean-cut gentleman," pointing to his short haircut.

"Ha, ha. Oh, what age does to a man ahh." Before Dan gets another word out, Paolo grabs him by the arm and pulls him toward a small café at the front-end of the building, where he buys two double espressos. After pouring considerable sugar in their cups, they down the black stimulants in seconds. The merger of sweet and bitter sensations on their tongues incites a conversation. They discuss small things, like sports. Both are huge Celtics fans, and most of the exchange revolves around Larry Bird.

"How is Francesca?"

"She's ahh fine. Thank you for asking. You know we would love if you came to the North End for dinner some night. It would be nice ahh...for the three of us to catch up...huh? Francesca sends her love ahh in the meantime."

"Well, give her my love, too. Dinner sounds fun. Let's do it. Perhaps this weekend...if you're available?"

"Yes ahh, we are. This will be fun. Let's ahh talk about it more after your presentation, OK? We don't want to be late. I know a lot of students and faculty are excited to hear ahh about your work." They slide off of their squeaky café stools, and Paolo leads Dan into the auditorium, a huge space with a cold draft and impersonal vibe. Dan mounts his black, plastic slide tray on the projector and turns the lamp on to test the focus. A few minutes later, the class starts filtering in, bringing the room to life.

After the group settles, Paolo introduces Dan. "Ladies and gentlemen...it is my pleasure to have my friend ahh...and colleague speak with us today. As you all know, he is a thought leader in the philosophy of psychology. Today he is ahh going to discuss his new work, entitled, *The Human Vessel – A Model for Interpersonal Interactions.*" It is a large group of nearly two hundred, all clustered in pockets throughout the room. They applaud loudly as Dan walks to the front.

"Thank you, Dr. Bettullio. I am so happy to be here. It is a true pleasure to talk with all these young, great minds. Let's start with this first slide. Can we dim the lights, please?" He clicks the controller, which forwards to an old photo of Paolo when he was a graduate student, holding a bottle of wine. "Oh no," Paolo screams over the laughter of the class. They are amused by his long, shoulder-length hair and bushy mustache, so fashionable in the hippy era in which he studied. Paolo jokingly scolds Dan by waving his index finger.

After the laughter from the first slide subsides, Dan provides the class with a steady stream of motivational energy, citing examples of how he became interested in philosophy and psychology. He then explains how logic, rhetoric, and psychology all coalesced in the development of his career, before reviewing the basis of his human vessel model and the significance of eastern philosophy in his thinking. To illustrate his points, he goes through slides with detailed schematics of vessels in various situations. When it appears that the students connect with his message, he steers the presentation toward an open dialogue at the sixty-minute time point.

"OK. Now, let's try to apply the vessel model to an actual situation. Does anyone have a real-life example that we may use?" From the front row, a tall, black student with thick, dark-rimmed glasses immediately raises his hand. Dan points to him, "Yes, sir. What are you thinking about?"

"Professor, how do you think your model applies to making acquaintances?"

"Oh, that's a great question. Are you referring to meeting people romantically or just in general?"

"I was thinking romantically, but it would be interesting if we could apply the question to both situations. I ask because I often find it difficult to make new friends here at BU."

Dan stands back on his heels and scratches his cheek. "Well, this is something I have been thinking a lot about lately, largely because I recently bumped into a person that has captured my imagination. Someone with whom I would like to get better acquainted. Anyway, so let's say you meet a stranger to whom you find yourself attracted. Beyond the physical attraction, you feel something deeper, a connection if you will. What is that sense? I mean, you don't even know the person, so what makes you gravitate to them? If we apply this situation to the human-vessel model, I think this is a condition in which the approached vessel has their energy ports opened. They are signaling, without uttering a single word, that it is safe to interact.

Hence, when you do interact, your energy starts to flow into their vessel, and vice versa. I think that is what we refer to as having chemistry with someone. It is all going on in our subconscious, instinctive brain. We have all experienced this sense. It gives us a feeling of connection, an elevated state of being." Dan leaves the area by the projector and walks closer to the young man. "The reverse is also true. You may approach a person who instead has their energy ports closed off to the world. They don't want to let you in, preferring to remain in their closed state. I mean, we all know one of the big reasons people act this way is because they have been hurt in the past, and they have now decided, consciously or unconsciously, not to allow any more potentially harmful energy in. In other words, any energy advance towards them is deflected away. I feel this is a sad emotional state. These vessels harbor the negative energy of past emotional pain, and they magnify those hurtful feelings by believing they can only count on themselves. The entire existence of a closed vessel is within—it's ego-driven. As a result, these closed vessels develop a sense of inflated ego, which just worsens their emotional health. My system would suggest that to connect with a closed vessel, you would need to be like a plumber of sorts, attempting to get through to them by opening their energy entry valves." He makes a twisting hand motion with an imaginary wrench to emphasize the point. "One way to do that is to have positive energy within your own vessel. Don't forget, they are also reading you. If they are sensing potential negative energy, they will just tighten their valves, and you will never connect. Relationships with closed vessels take a long time to evolve, and when they do, it allows the closed vessel to taste the beauty of having another person to be open with, thereby normalizing their inner energy and emotional health. Does that make any sense?" The young man nods, seemingly satisfied with Dan's response.

A few more thoughts spin into Dan's head and he continues. "Then, I think there are times when we aren't sure how to act. Like the other day when I met this person that I was attracted to, I actually had my own energy get trapped within. What I'm trying to say is I wanted to reach out, but I had such inner turmoil, that I couldn't. It was as if my energy was just stuck, bouncing back and forth within my being–kind of like emotional constipation. I think this often happens when you try too hard...when you want something too much. You just want to let your energy spill out and take control of a situation–but instead, the harder you try, the less effective the outcome. It's like picking up a handful of sand." He makes a fist. "The more forcibly you squeeze, the more the granules fall to the ground. Just passively holding the sand in your palm allows it to remain. If we would just keep our inflow and outflow valves open, the energy will naturally diffuse in the appropriate directions. We must trust the fundamental flow of things. I realize this is easy to say and acknowledge that it's much more difficult to do. I think maintaining a disciplined mind is the best way to achieve optimal emotional connections. The bottom line is, just let relationships happen...don't force them." Dan raises his arms over his head in a sun salutation-like gesture.

He surveys the class. They're nodding agreeably.

Paolo stands from his chair and walks to the front of the room to moderate the question-and-answer period.

An eager, skinny girl dressed in a yellow sport shirt

with a crocodile logo stands at the microphone. "Professor, thank you very much for your presentation. I am curious about the vessel itself. Is this something genetic, or do we become it, in sort of an existential fashion?"

"Well, that is another wonderful point. First, I would like to say, that I do subscribe to Sartre's idea that 'Existence precedes essence.' Given that our existence is in part biological, I would have to say that to some extent, our vessel dynamic is regulated at a genetic level. Nevertheless, like everything else in our lives, we can use our higher-end cognitive abilities to regulate and file incoming energy within the context of that genetic background. Our mental capacities can regulate what energies flow inward and register with our emotions. Hence, I believe we can carve out the essence of our individual vessels on the backdrop of our biology. If a toxic event sends negative energy my way, I can choose to open my outflow valve even more so, providing egress for that toxic energy. Moreover, I can also detoxify whatever negative energy enters my vessel. In that part of the model, I would allow the toxic energy in, but transform or neutralize it before it was able to influence me. We need to be both transformers and plumbers, right?" The group laughs. After a few more student questions, Paolo announces "OK, we ahh...have time for one more ahh."

Dr. Ezekiel Rimrodder stands and shuffles to the microphone. Dan thought Rimrodder would likely attend and try to disrupt his presentation as he's done so many times at national society meetings. Rimrodder was the department chair at BU before Paolo stepped in and replaced him. He established his long academic career in philosophical ethics, writing extensively on the moral superiority of Old Testament values. Paolo dislikes him as much as Dan, and was just about to cut him off from asking his question, when Rimrodder taps the microphone in a smug, arrogant manner. He is wearing a blue-striped polo shirt tucked into pleated khakis. A thick, red belt with a gold buckle holds his outfit together. It pushes a ring of belly fat down toward his knees, making him resemble a walrus. He again taps the microphone while simultaneously bringing his pasty lips toward it. "Sir, that was such a cute presentation. I am quite sure students, like my African American friend in the first row, appreciated the obvious analogies presented here today. I must say, however, that I am finding your entire system weak on the side of scholarship. I mean the banality of covering how to meet people is not a suitable topic for philosophy in higher education. I am not sure how you get away with such low-level academic pursuits at your elite university across the river."

Paolo starts to cut the banter off, but before he could, Dan interjects, "No, please, Dr. Bettullio, I am more than happy to have Dr. Rimrodder express his thoughts.

"It's Rimrodder...with a long O."

Dan responds, "Yes...yes, so sorry, Dr. Rimrodder." He again enunciates the short O...and is sure to emphasize the mispronunciation.

Paolo asks, "Professor, do you have a question?"

"I do, Dr. Bettullio. Thank you. Sir, have you thought about how your model may fit into national security? In other words, in your philosophy, could a country also be modeled as a vessel?"

"Yes, I believe it could."

"Well, do you think that all country vessels should have

the same international standing? It is very clear that many countries hold dark and dangerous viewpoints. Places like the Soviet Union and North Korea should not be trusted with a natural flow of the world's energy as you put it. Would you agree that those vessels need to be limited and prevented from expansion?"

"Well, quite frankly, I find that to be a concerning view. I think that the audience should be aware of our lingering debate regarding US foreign interventionism."

"Sir, I am quite sure these students have read my work." He slowly looks over the auditorium.

"Well, then it should be clear to them that you have used philosophy as a very dangerous tool. Many, including me, feel your misguided thinking of placing US interests above the rest of the worlds is criminal. Especially, since you have advised the last three Republican administrations on such topics."

In a measured voice, Rimrodder responds, "Sir, life is not so Pollyanna. If we didn't have the moral fortitude to protect Judeo-Christian ethics and freedom throughout the world, there would just be chaos. The dark forces of communism would spread and destroy our way of life. Not all peoples are created equal. This is very clear in the Old Testament. Your post-modern, energy transfer methodology cannot work in the real world."

"Dr. Rimrodder, I simply reject the premise behind your imperialistic views. The Roman Empire went down that road centuries ago, and they collapsed from within—their vessel empire imploded. We need to strive toward a global, peaceful coexistence. Anything short of that will likely cause this country to collapse, in the same vein as the Romans. Our biggest threat as a civilization stems from people like you. Those who want to build more bombs and issue more threats. Those that are desperate to control the narrative. Also, and I say this with as much respect as I can muster, I feel the hegemonic policies in which you have played an integral role, are nothing more than a capitalistic ploy for the military-industrial complex."

"I beg your pardon. I'm finding your tone discourteous. Certainly, not fitting for a guest speaker."

"So be it, Professor Rimrodder. I am not here to appease your shortsighted, malignant worldview. One of the nuances of my model...is that when one vessel tries to bully another vessel, the latter can also negate the former's ability to spill their poison. See, bullies feel insignificant, so when they attempt to push their energy on the rest of us, to make themselves feel more important, we can stop them at point zero. Please, let me say publicly, that I will not allow you to infuse your toxins in my presence. I will just not let you. I am bigger than that...a bigger person than you. You don't get to control the situation. You don't get to base your deplorable philosophies on biblical writings. It's beyond hypocritical. You talk about scholarship...may I suggest that you no longer use the Bible as a scholarly reference. It was never intended as such." Dan was doing his best to stay calm, despite his puffed-out chest and raised voice.

"So much for letting the energy flow on its own," issues Rimrodder in a spiteful tone.

"Yes, so much for that," responds Dan.

Paolo waves his hand and stops the exchange. "Thank you for such a spirited discourse, gentleman. This was a very interesting session. It has...ahh...given us much to contemplate."

Dan takes a deep breath and thanks the group for their attention. The class applauds and starts to disperse, except for Rimrodder who goes back to his seat and starts writing something in a black notebook. He has a full-toothed smile.

Paolo turns the lights brighter while Dan clears his slides from the projector. As he positions the slide tray back in its box, he looks through the disassembling students exiting the room. Then in the ultimate irony, he thinks he sees Chiara walking out of a rear door. To himself, "No it can't be...my eyes must be..." He quickly runs to the back of the room to get a closer look, while dodging a few extra-diligent students soliciting career advice. When he gets to the doorway, SHE is nowhere to be found.

"Dan, Dan...Where are you going?" asks Paolo as he tries to catch up. "Is ahh, everything all right?"

"Yes...yes...fine. I just thought I recognized someone back here. I must have made a mistake."

In an out of breath voice, "I've ahh, never seen you move so fast."

"Ha, ha. Yeah, I used to be fast like that when I played ball."

Paolo asks, "Are you feeling all right? Your presentation was ahh really fantastic. Rimrodder didn't make you upset, did he?"

"Oh, thanks. Yeah...yes, I'm fine," Dan says, playing off his preoccupation with the coincidence he had just experienced. No...no, even though I can't stand the little imbecile, he doesn't have the capacity to make me upset."

"I know, I can't stand him either. The students complain all the time ahh. He's always trying to date the women in his classes. He thinks he's a real Don Juan ahh because of his political connections." Paolo makes a pinecone hand gesture.

"Yeah, it must be those khakis." They both laugh heartily.

Turning to a serious face, Paolo says, "I have been meaning to ask ahh...how have you been doing since your divorce? I was hoping we could talk ahh."

They move to a private area in the hallway. A few seconds elapse. This is the first time Paolo has made such an inquiry, and Dan isn't sure how to react. "Thanks for asking. I'm doing all right. It hasn't been easy...it's hard to bury the dead, you know."

Paolo pauses, and in a consoling fashion squeezes his arm. "Another love ahh...will come along for you soon. You're a good man."

"That may be, but true love, like you and Francesca... well, it's almost impossible to find."

Paolo's eyes beam with kindness. "You know, I'm ahh sorry for not being there more for you. I never knew what to say...our friendship with Taylor too...I'm ahh so sorry."

"I know. It's OK. I understand that you were caught in the middle."

"Francesca has been in touch with Taylor on several occasions. I never know how to react ahh."

"Yeah, well...I'm glad they're still friends." Dan smirks at the irony of it all. Their conversation gradually tapers as Paolo escorts him out of the building. Before opening the double-glass door to the street, Dan reaches out to shake Paolo's hand. "Thanks for inviting me."

Paolo responds with another strong, jovial hug. "My pleasure, my friend, grazie mille." Before closing the door,

Dan pauses...wanting to ask Paolo about Chiara. Instead, he buries his thoughts into his side pockets, like a shy boy does with his hands in uncertain situations. "Arrivederci, I'll call you tomorrow to make plans for dinner."

"OK. Ciao, thanks again."

As Dan walks away from BU, he finds himself back on Comm Ave heading east through Kenmore Square. He ponders his presentation, his talk with Paolo, Rimrodder, and Chiara. He knows he must see HER again—it's in his DNA. Should he go back to the gallery a third time? That would be blatantly obvious, but maybe being obvious would be the best approach.

~ 2 ~

Delano

Today's Del's big day. He's extra excited to present his science report to the 5th-grade class. He wants to look good and wakes up early to take a bath. After dressing in his dark-brown corduroy suit, he smooths out the wrinkles in the big lapels and meticulously combs his hair. Proudly, he walks into the kitchen where he finds his mom drinking coffee and reading the newspaper. "Oh, don't you look handsome today, honey. I made you some eggs and toast." Del has never done a presentation before and has a nervous stomach. "I'm not hungry. I think I'll just have a slice of toast."

"OK, here you go."

Del's father enters the kitchen. "So, are you prepared, Del?"

"Yes, I think so. Last night while you were at work, I rehearsed a few times."

"Well, that's good. You can never practice too much to achieve excellence."

"That's for sure."

"Be sure to speak slowly and to enunciate your words clearly. Remember...show the class that you are confident about your work." He rubs his hand over Del's head. Del fixes his hair when he finishes.

"I'll try my best."

"Come here, I have to go...give me a kiss. I'm proud of you."

"Thanks, Dad."

As Del finishes his toast, his mother points to the clock and says, "Honey, you better hurry. You don't want to be late for your big day."

"OK. I'm leaving now. I should be at the bus stop right on time."

"I'll see you after school. Don't forget your lunch. I put in a slice of apple pie for a special treat." They hug goodbye before she kisses his forehead. "Go get 'em, Tiger."

Del walks down the block and waits for the school bus at the corner of his street. He stays away from the other kids playing tag on a neighbor's lawn because he doesn't want to get dirty. Instead, he stands alone on the corner, mentally rehearsing some of the key facts of his presentation. When the squeaky-braked bus arrives, he climbs aboard. Before he even reaches his seat, a couple of kids sitting in the rear start whistling and jeering at him for wearing a suit. "Del's a brown, shitty-looking sissy. Del's a brown, shitty-looking sissy," they say. He ignores them. Chuckie, the kid in the group that Del dislikes the most, raises the stakes by pulling Del's hair. After a few tugs, Del calmly gets up, and moves to a seat in the front of the bus. Not happy with not being able to get on Del's nerves, Chuckie then tries plan B, which consists of shooting spitballs at Del's head. "Settle down...Charles," yells the bus driver when she sees what is happening. Chuckie and the boys don't listen. They continue to scorch him.

After a big wet one hits his right ear, Del feels himself starting to turn into that other person he sometimes becomes—the one that scares him. As the bus pulls into the school drop-off area, Del rises from his seat and walks toward the boys. "Sit down, Del," yells the driver. Del ignores her command. He instead runs feverishly towards Chuckie, where he grabs his neck and slams his lunch pail into his large watermelon-like head. Chuckie's nose squirts blood. The other kids scream. Del maliciously asks, "Who's the brown-sissy now, Chuckie-boy?" Chuckie's friends cower in their seats.

The next thing Del knows, he is suspended from school. His mother and father pick him up. They say nothing during the eternal car ride home.

At home, they sit around the kitchen table. "What happened?"

He explains.

His father says, "So, why did you let that kid stop you from making a great presentation?"

"Honey, fighting never solves anything," follows his mother.

"I know. I just snapped. I don't even know what happened."

His father stands and points his finger at his forehead. "Young man, I'm only going to say this once. Work on controlling your temper. You are grounded for two weeks. In the meantime, you will write an apology to Charles and his parents. Then you will write separate apologies to your principal and bus driver. They need to know you will not act like this again."

Del starts to complain, but his father cuts him off. "Don't even say another..." Del stops mid-sentence. "Lastly, go get your book report. You will present it to us right now."

Del trudges out of the room and comes back a few minutes later with two paper-clipped pages—on the first page, a typed-out version of the presentation—on the second, a sketch of a Monarch butterfly, colored appropriately in orange and black crayon.

Monarch Butterflies by Del P.
Monarch butterflies are very interesting creatures. They have very beautiful orange and black wings. They also have some white spots. They are easy to find here in Pennsylvania. We only get to see them in the late summer though. Their wings are about 4 inches wide. They fly very gracefully and land on our flowers. Sometimes my dog chases them, but he can never catch them because they fly so fast.

Monarch butterflies go through many changes in their lives. This process is called metamorphosis. First, they start out as an egg and live on plant leaves. They then hatch and become caterpillars. Many caterpillars are killed by predators. The ones that survive then learn to weave, like my mom. They make a soft bed of silk, and wrap themselves in it, upside down!

They stay there for about two weeks. I know how they feel because sometimes I wish I could stay in my bed for two weeks too. When they are in the silk, they are in the pupa stage. After that, they crawl out of the pupa and learn to fly. That is when they become adult butterflies. In the winter, they migrate to warm places like Mexico, which is very far. I do not know how they do not get tired flying so far. I also do not know how they know where they are going. They go through so many changes in their lives. Monarch butterflies are such amazing creatures.

~~~

Zach

I can't believe a year has passed since I started working with Pergo. I gotta say, he's really helped me. At least now, I can identify my triggers and can pretty much control my outbursts. I don't go down to the Combat Zone anymore. I think he's right; I need to get back to basics and maintain clear barriers in my life. I've redirected my paintings to focus on outdoor themes and landscapes. Yesterday, I did an 18 X 24 of a couple sharin' a picnic in front of the Hatch Shell with the Charles in the background. I included some bicyclists, rollerbladers, and sailboats to capture the constant activity around that place. I think it turned out OK. Anyway, at my last session, Pergo told me that he thought I was doing pretty well, and it would be appropriate if we started taperin' down our sessions. At first, I thought he was gettin' sick of me, but then after thinkin' about it more, I realized it was his cue for me to start gettin' on with my life. He suggested it would be a good time for me to travel a little and maybe take a weekend trip for a change of scenery. So, for the first time in a couple of years, I'm goin' to head north and do some paintin' along coastal Maine. I have a reservation at a place
~~~

that I used to stay at near Camden. Luckily, they had an openin'.

After organizin' some things like my toothbrush, clothes, and a flashlight, I pack my French easel. I throw a few big tubes of oil, along with a jug of terpenoid, into a burlap bag and struggle down my apartment steps with all the gear. Bein' an artist requires a lot of baggage. After returnin' two more times to load the freshly stretched canvases in the rear, I trek back upstairs to lock the door before gettin' on my way.

It's obvious after only two minutes of bein' on the road that people are drivin' like they're crazy. It prompts me to keep a heavy foot on the brake. Weavin' east to the Tobin, I pass through Bunker Hill where the traffic isn't too bad. I open the window for some fresh air and scroll through a bunch of radio stations before findin' Marley. I turn up the volume and start singin' along. A couple of cars next to me notice the karaoke, but they don't dissuade me—'cause I sing my way right across the Tobin into Chelsea, holdin' my position in the center lane.

Sippin' on a coffee, I watch the road signs move from the windshield to the rear-view. Camden's a long drive, but worth the effort. I can't wait to get to the small cabin that I rented. It's on a remote part of the Penobscot Bay, a little south of town. You know, it's nothin' fancy, but it's got a gorgeous perspective to paint from. Like I said, I stayed there the last time I was up that way. I also like that it's close to the great elevated vantage points at Camden Hills State Park. My landscapes are going to be big, very big—just like Mount Battie.

After a couple hours of drivin', I pull over at Freeport to refill my coffee at a Starbucks. I sit at a small table next to a mom and her two kids. The older kid looks about three and is a cutey. I can't stop admirin' her sharin' pieces of a blueberry muffin with her little sister, who is still in diapers. As they wash down their tiny morsels with hot chocolate, they ask their mom a thousand questions, who while straddlin' three shoppin' bags from the Calvin Klein outlet, continually strokes their long blonde strands behind their tiny ears, patiently answerin' every one of 'em. Her nurturing bathes the children like the summer sun. I think the love small children feel must be a perfect love, but I'm only guessin'.

Next to the kids sits an older couple in matchin' button-down sweaters. They're sippin' Frappuccinos from long plastic cups, breaking up the condensation of icy sugar with even longer straws. They talk, engagin' each other like they just met. Probin' one another's thoughts, they lean slightly forward. Their gold weddin' bands suggest a history, and they have the same content look in their eyes as the little girls. Maybe all love is perfect...but again, who the F' knows.

I finish my coffee and walk back towards the truck, where I turn right out of the parkin' lot and head north. I arrive at the cabin by two and pull over at the converted farmhouse check-in area, where I find a husky girl wearing an oversized white sweatshirt, readin' *Bon Appetite.* She a looks up from a peach pie recipe and gives me a nice smile when I enter.

"Hello."

"Hi, I'm Zach Fostaa...checkin' in."

"Welcome, Zach. We're so glad you decided to come back and stay with us again."

"Thanks. It's good to be baack."

"How was the traffic?"

"Not too baad."

"That's good to hear. Your trip is off to a good start then." She hands me a key fastened to a green wooden holder with #6 scratched in the middle. "Your cabin is just around the bend over there...to the left." She points. "Please, if you need anything at all, feel free to call me. I'm always here. My name is Alyssa."

"I will. Thanks, AAlyssaa."

On my way out, "Oh, and Zach, please don't leave any garbage or food outside—the animals and everything. Oh yeah...and here's a 20% off coupon for a boat ride at the harbor." She gets up from her tiny desk and hands me the yellow coupon.

"That's nice—thanks again. I'll be sure to clean up after myself."

"Enjoy Camden."

I get back in the truck and drive slowly down the small dirt road toward the cabin. I find #6 in the middle of ten or so similar brownish-green structures aligned around the inlet. I'm able to park close to the door with only a few steps on a grey shell pathway to unload my stuff.

I enter the simple one room space consistin' of a kitchenette and a single bed situated under a large bay window facin' the water. I pull my bags inside and place 'em in a small closet with a door that looks like an accordion. Alyssa left a welcome basket on the counter for me. It's filled with bottles of fruit juice and small snack bags of nuts and chips, with a card—PLEASE ENJOY YOUR STAY, ZACH. I grab a bag of almonds and a juice and go outside to explore.

On the small, quiet beach, I find some scattered green

Adirondack chairs and a fire pit. I recline on one of 'em and rest my legs on a big stone while washin' a few almonds down with OJ. I light a small fire with thin pieces of birch that I found layin' around the wooded fringes of the parkin' lot. Starin' at the flames, I can't help savorin' the cool, salty sea air mixed with the smoky-sweet aromas of the wood. It feels nice. After an hour or so, a steady and thick, blue fog starts to settle in. Like ghosts, the mist and clouds tell stories of the past. Whalers and shipbuilders project across the horizon like characters on a giant drive-in movie screen. I think it's nature's way of tellin' us things.

***

Two hours later, I get hungry and decide to drive into town for dinner. When I arrive, I park on top of a small hill near the public library overlookin' the harbor. Town is just as nice as I remember. The streets are lined with colonial houses and have white picket fences, tulip gardens, and trellises with purple clematis. There's also a bunch of small shops and cafés. They're all filled up with people havin' dinner and drinks. Along the water, next to the boat excursion companies jockeyin' for tourists, sits a few seafood shacks. I find my way over to one and order from a fat guy workin' the window. "Yeah, how 'bout a cold lagaa and a steamed lobstaa...please." He looks disgusted and wipes his hands on his apron, "OK, sport. I'm busy; just wait a minute." I smile and watch his words float to the sky like a balloon. My meal comes with sides of corn-on-the-cob, coleslaw, french fries, and a wedge of greenish-yellow lemon. I enjoy every morsel, even dippin' my fries in the butter.

After I eat, I walk around the area to scope out some potential paintin' topics. I like the perspective from the library, capturin' some of the schooners. I take out my sketchpad and freehand. The sun has almost fully set, and I feel alive with possibilities. I decide to sleep on 'em till I get an early start with the brushes tomorrow. It's always easier to make decisions in the mornin'.

I go back to the truck and navigate toward the cabin in the opposite direction. After a few lefts, I find myself on a two-lane road for about five miles before makin' another left onto the dirt path that merges into the inlet. Pebbles ricochet against my truck, and the cracklin' sounds of my tires against the stony surface are amplified by the silence of pitch-black darkness. It's a little eerie here, and I'm cautious on my way to the door. It takes me five minutes of fiddlin' with the key to get inside, and when I do, I quickly flip the switch of the wobbly lamp standing at the side of the bed. The cool night air is pervadin' the small gaps in the walls, leavin' me with a chill. I reach into my bag and pull out an old sweatshirt to sleep in. I also keep the lamp on as I drift off. I have that dream again.

"I pledge allegiance to the flag....to the Republic...one nation under God..."

"OK class, please turn in your homework."

I have nothin'.

"Zach, where is your paper?"

I say nothin'. It's rainin' outside and the wataa paaralyzes me.

"Zach, I'm talking to you. Do you want to go see the

Monsignor again?" I shivaa. Silence has come ovaa the other children.

"That's it. Get to the office."

I wait for ten minutes before his door opens. There he is. He greets me by slowly liftin' his bald head. Through his bushy eyebrows, I see the ugly gaze.

"Come in, Zachary. Why were you sent here?"

"I didn't do my homework...sir."

"Young man, how many times do I have to tell you that to be a productive member of society, you have to be responsible and respect authority? You just do not seem to want to listen...do you? Let's go through our priorities. Please recite them."

I take a deep breath. Old Spice and sweat fill the flat aair. "God first...country second...family third, sir."

"All right. Do you know that you are violating all of our priorities...by not being responsible for your work?"

"Yes, Monsignaa...I'm..."

"So, why do you keep doing it? You leave me no choice but to help you remember."

"Please Monsignaa, not again, I'm..."

I feel the burning. His shaarpness cuts me while I stare at the flag hangin' in the cornaa.

His pace picks up and the jostlin' of my head causes the red, white, and blue to blur. "That's right, son. This will help you remember."

I feel dirty.

He smirks at me when he places the communion host on my tongue that Sunday. I spit it out when I return to the pew. No one sees, because they're all distracted—staarin' at the altaa—like they see somethin' special.

I wake up in a sweat. God, I hate thinkin' about it. That set of foster parents were nice enough when they weren't drinkin'. I relive the pain, the itch. I again wonder who my real parents are. I lie back down and doze off, restlessly, until I'm reawakened by the hum of a red and silver lobster boat trollin' its lines. Despite my dream, I feel alert and energetically get out of bed. It's 6 AM on a sunny Saturday, and I want to get back to town while the mornin' light is right.

I park in the same spot as I did last night. I cart my gear down the hill and stop at a tiny café for a take-out coffee. I pay with some loose change, leaving a few quarters for a tip. Under his five-day-old scruff and Bruins cap, the college kid servin' me smiles at my austerity.

You're welcome young man.

I walk back outside and set up my easel near a little waterfall between the main street and the harbor. I study it and get connected. Around the water sits a bunch of interestin' rocks and flowers, creating contrasts of light interspersed with deep shadows. I sketch the scene and get into it quickly. It's a small canvas, and I finish it in a few hours. I feel pretty good about it. Some tourist types compliment me as I clean off my brushes in the turpenoid.

I start to get hungry, and after wipin' the remnant colors from my hands, I buy a few fried clams from one of the nearby shacks, where I squeeze lemon all over their crunchy skins. Sittin' on a wooden bench lookin' at the boats, I chow on the small golden morsels, pullin' them from the paper bowl with a pointy, wooden stick.

A few benches away, I notice this Asian girl readin' intently. She is sitting cross-legged in a comfortable posture and seems to have an openness about her. She also looks smokin' hot, so I get up to check 'er out. Tryin' to inconspicuously decipher the title of her book, I almost fall over when I realize it's a pocket Bible. *Holy Shit...she's too young to be interested in biblical fantasia.* I feel the hairs on the back of my neck standin' on end and wish I could go over and rip it out of her hands. As I begin to recognize my thought escalation, I calm down and become present.

OK...that's her choice...maybe it gives her purpose...I'm gonna go talk with 'er...I mean, Pergo keeps tellin' me to try to put myself out there...with normal...

"Excuse me...ahh Miss...but I notice that you're reading the Bible." She glances upwards with her large, almond eyes. She has a slight swipe of mascara across the top outside corners of her lashes but is otherwise not made-up. The natural warmth of her apple-shaped cheeks is welcoming. "I'm sorry for being so forward, but can I ask you what you gain from reading it?"

Without pause, "It provides peace and wisdom in my life."

My instinct is to start debating the basis of religion with her, but my urge is quenched by her obvious authenticity. Besides, she doesn't need some stranger infiltrating her tranquility with his bias against God.

But did Moses really part the Red Sea? Give me a break...I breathe...I breathe...I breathe.

She breaks my cynical thought escalation when she asks me if I have faith.

"Oh, not really. Well, I was raised religious, but now...no...I'm not part of anything now."

"Why the change?"

"Well, it's complicated. You know, situations...stuff just...kind of happened." I try to change the topic.

She senses my reservations but continues anyway. “I think everyone has doubts. For me, it’s natural to question the literality of the Bible. But to meditate over the metaphysics of creation, eternity, life, death, love, and forgiveness is really what it’s about.” The words roll off her tongue with ease and clarity. Normally, I would have run for the hills, but there is something about her.

She fixes her hair, clears her throat, and continues. “Even though I can’t intellectualize it, I feel connected to my faith. I think that’s the important part of it all—being connected and knowing that even in death you will evolve into a new birth at some other level. Jesus gave us that gift. He gave us grace.”

Her eloquent steadiness is impressive. I feel a sense of peace with her words. “Wow, this is a really heavy conversation for not knowing one anothaa.”

“Yeah, it is.”

“So, what’s your name?”

“I’m Megan.”

“Nice to meet you. I’m Zach.” We shake hands. Hers is warm and soft.

“What do you do, Zach? You don’t get paid to interview people about the books they’re reading, do you?” She smiles.

At first, I don’t catch the sarcasm. With a slight delay, “I’m an aartist. See, I just did that paintin’.” I point over to it. She gets up from the bench to take a closer look.

“That’s just beautiful.”

“Thanks...”

“When I see art like this, I know there’s a God. You just did her work.”

“Well, I...” She cuts me off. “You are really talented.

Have you shown anything?"

"Yeah, I've had a bunch of gallery shows and even a..." I catch myself.

"Wow, that's impressive. So, how long have you been painting here? I've never seen you before."

"Oh, today's the first day...I'm up here from Boston. I want to capture some of these fantastic landscapes." I widely spread my arms out toward the water.

"How 'bout you, how long are you visitin'?"

"Oh, I live here. My parents run a bed and breakfast a few miles up the road. I came back after graduating from college last year. Right now, I'm doing some part-time graduate classes while helping them out at the B & B."

"Really, where'd you go?

"I went to Penn. In Philly."

"I heard that's a wicked good school. Do you like being baack?"

"Yeah...mostly, but it gets a little boring sometimes. Almost all of my friends have moved out of the area to exciting cities, like New York. I do love the quiet mystique of Camden, though."

"Me too. This is one of the most spectaculaa places. It makes me feel free."

"Did you study art in college?"

"Yeah, I went to the school of haard knocks. Ha, ha."

"Well, you definitely didn't go to comedy school. That's for sure." She belts out an even bigger laugh.

Oh...a witty one.

"So, where are you staying?"

"In a cabin down the road." I describe its location, and she tells me she used to swim around there when she was a kid. We talk for another hour about all sorts of things, like Picasso, Faneuil Hall, and cheesesteaks.

As our conversation tapers, she says, "Well, I have to get going to help my parents get set up for some guests. It was very nice talking with you."

"It was very nice talking with you too. Hey, umm Megaan, do you want to maybe...ummm, meet up anothaa time for a cup of coffee or somethin'?"

Shit, this is a milestone for me. I'm proud of myself.

"I would love that," she says. "Are you free tomorrow morning? I could meet you after church."

"Perfect."

"How about we meet at this bench around eleven thirty. That will give me a chance to help my folks with brunch after mass."

As we part, she gives me a slight hug—the kind I've seen friends give. I holler as she walks away, "It was really nice to meet you...Megaan."

It's late afternoon and I decide to head back to the cabin after packin' up my stuff. On my way, I stop at a little store and buy a steak to grill over the fire pit. I eat facin' the water while chewin' on the sunset. I swallow its brilliance while thinkin' about 'er.

"Hey, to all you guys out theaa. Now, I know what you're thinkin'...how could this guy be doin' so well when he's such a nutjob? Who frickin' knows? Didn't anyone evaa teach ya that rollin' your eyes is impolite?"

~~~

Dan

The next morning, Dan picks up the phone and dials Paolo. After a few rings, Paolo answers with a distracted affect. "Pronto."
~~~

"Hey, Paolo, it's Dan. I just wanted to thank you again for inviting me last evening."

"My friend. This was my pleasure."

"So, I'm calling to ask if you and Francesca still want to have dinner this weekend."

"Oh, yes ahh...Dan, this would be wonderful! We discussed it last ahh night."

"I was thinking that we go to The Daily Catch for lobster fra diavolo and calamari. You know how I love it there."

"Perfetto...we do too. It reminds us of a little trattoria that we used to go to in Roma, where they also serve the pasta in the pan ahh—stove to table. How's...tomorrow at six? Looking forward to it, we will find a place ahh in line ahh. Meet you there...a presto."

"Grazie." Dan hangs up the phone and feels happy to have something to do on a Saturday night. He darts downstairs to pick up the *Globe* after doing a few push-ups and sit-ups, and reads over a breakfast of hardboiled eggs, sprinkled with a heavy coating of black pepper. He quickly becomes disgusted with the front-page article on the Iran-Contra affair. He knows it was orchestrated from the very top, with advice from war hawks like Rimrodder. He folds the eggshells into the paper and tosses them both into the garbage. He has no further appetite for political deceit.

He thinks about doing some writing and redirects his attention to his journal. Like always, he pauses to collect his thoughts before poking the paper with his sharp pencil. Scribbled on the top of the page is a quote from Kafka. *'A book must be the axe for the frozen sea within us.'* After a few quiet minutes, he starts chopping a passage of his own.

Was seeing her a coincidence? What about my dream—me rescuing her? I'm not sure coincidences even exist. All I know is she is pulling at me. Those green eyes—intoxicating absinthe. But what can I offer in return? I'm just an empty vessel with nothing more than smoke and mirror illusions of being significant. I can't contaminate her young life; she doesn't deserve my dirt. Maybe it's time to leave this fantasy behind. Act or not—we all end up alone.

***

The next evening, Dan picks up the T from Copley to Government Center. He cuts down the steps toward Haymarket and courses through the outdoor market. It's cleanup time, and he is careful to avoid the boxes and wooden crates that litter the stone pavement. As he does, he also holds his nose from the rancid, vinegar-like stench of the garbage dumpsters. Darting around clumps of rotting vegetables and scattered oyster shells, he passes a few Chinese women with large pushcarts haggling vendors for extra eggplants and broccoli—already discounted ten for a dollar. It's a typical Saturday night and people are bustling around everywhere.

After making it past the market, he crosses over to the North End where he is greeted by the pleasant aromas of basil and garlic. After a few blocks, he meets Paolo and Francesca outside the restaurant, midway down Hanover. They're drinking Chianti in plastic wine cups while holding a place in the front of a long line, nearly one block long. Dan joins them by giving Francesca two kisses on each of her highly set cheeks.

"Buonasera. You look fantastic, Dan," she says.

"It's so great to see you."

"Yes, it's ahh been too long.

"You haven't aged a bit, Francesca; you still have the most beautiful skin in Boston. I know, it's the olive oil, right? Ha, ha...Please, I brought you some roses from the flower garden." Dan offers the small bouquet to her. She graciously accepts the flowers and holds the petals to her nose in a delicate, appreciative manner. Her long, chestnut brown hair is fixed into a bun secured with a jeweled clip. She has small, dark eyes that look like raisins, and a lean straight posture with gently rounded muscular shoulders, developed from her years of ballet.

She and Paolo first met in their early twenties after her premier as Cinderella at the Teatro dell'Opera di Roma. As the story goes, Paolo became so taken with her performance, he waited for her outside the opera house for two hours after the show. When she finally strolled out, he didn't use a cliché Prince Charming introduction, but instead a straightforward pledge that his 'heart was forever hers.' It worked, and they have been together ever since. When they moved from Rome two years later, Francesca became the prima ballerina at the Boston Ballet. Dan and Taylor used to love watching her dance. Her beauty and grace were captivating.

"Oh, Dan ahh, you are still a charmer huh...che bei fiores...thank you..."

"Also, I thought you might enjoy this pocket-sized copy of *Paradiso*. I know how much you enjoy poetry." He hands it to her.

"You are so ahh kind, thank you. I love it." She gives him another kiss, this time on only one cheek. Paolo pours a cup of wine for him. Dan holds it up and offers a toast. "To old friends. May your days continue to be filled with infinite love, and your nights with infinite passion...Cin, cin."

"Oh, grazie."

"Salute." They tap their glasses. Behind them are two middle-aged couples talking with soft, southern drawls. They politely acknowledge the toast by tipping their beer cans. A group of college girls, next in line to be seated, start to loudly slur "Cheers" as they refill their tall cups with white wine from a brown paper bag. They are catching glances from the entire street in their short skirts and high heels. Tourists carrying large cameras and bulky fanny packs cause congestion along the sidewalk. Even though shotgun sounds from taxis and Harleys make it difficult to talk, two older women sitting on a corner bench are having no problem conversing in Italian—their hands gesturing vigorously.

"My pleasure...Francesca."

"I like ahh your shoes," she says.

"Thanks, I just bought them..."

Just then, the waitress sticks her head out of the industrial glass door and yells, "Bethany, table for six." The college girls chug their wine and scoot to their seats. "Paolo, party for three." Paolo puts his arm around Dan and Francesca and guides them to the door in a fatherly manner. Fortunately, they secure a window table, providing a great view of people funneling in and out of Mike's Pastries across the street. They are also relieved that they're not sitting too close to the college girls, who are already asking for more bread and toasting to "Passion" with another cup of wine.

"Francesca, it has been too long. It is so good to see

you. Are you still running your dance studio in Beacon Hill?"

"I am. I can't believe that I've been in business for almost ten years ahh. My life seems to be passing by so fast ahh. I am even thinking about opening another in Brookline. So many young girls want to dance."

"Well, they all just want to train with the best prima ballerina ever."

Francesca smiles politely. "How ahh about you? How are you feeling since the divorce? Are you seeing anyone?"

Dan knows that Francesca will likely tell Taylor everything they discuss, so he answers with a humorous digression, "Everyone I can, Francesca...everyone I can." He internally sneers, as he hasn't been on a date since the break-up. The waitress trudges over to the table. "What-a-you-guys havin'?"

"Oh...lets ahh start with the fried calamari," says Paolo.

"Yes, and an order of the calamari meatballs too," adds Dan. Paolo refreshes their glasses as the waitress leans over the stainless-steel counter to place their order.

"Dan ahh, Paolo tells me you did a fantastic presentation this week. He explained some of your ideas to me. It sounds like you are developing something very interesting."

"Well, I'm still kind of working through it all. I've just been trying to think about how energy is transferred between people during interpersonal exchanges." He nods towards her.

"What do you mean by this? I'm ahh not following."

"Well, let's see...for example, think about your relationships with your dance partners. I'm sure you have danced better with some compared to others. I would guess that those differences weren't necessarily physical... but instead related to something intangible. That's the energy part." Dan extends his arms toward the window. "It's like a feeling or an intuition between people that we can't place our finger on. That's sort of what it's about."

"What ahh about these vessels? Paolo tried to explain them to me, but I don't understand."

"Well, they are just sort of a visual aid. Think of each of us as individual clusters of energy, sort of a shell of energy encased by skin."

She studies his face as he speaks. "OK."

"Then when people add or subtract energy from their individual vessel, it results in personality shifts. For example, when Taylor and I were married, we shared everything, like you and Paolo do now. Instead of individual small vessels, couples merge into a large, shared vessel. One that holds a lot of energy. Now you and Paolo still have this great constant renewable energy, exchanging it back and forth between your two compartments as needed." He looks at Paolo. "This, I think of as love...a high energy situation. The two of you are much bigger than your individual parts. Conversely, when couples split, their shared vessel hemorrhages—letting all the energy spill out. It can leave a us with sense of smallness...we become low energy creatures."

"Fried calamari."

"Yes, grazie, just in the middle," says Francesca. "Can we have some bread too, please?"

Dan dips a large purple tentacle in the spicy gravy. "Or think about when you retired from the ballet. The troupe was part of you, and you left a piece of yourself with the other dancers. I suspect that you felt that loss of energy and perhaps...filled that void with opening your studio. Individual purpose is like a siphon that pulls energy in."

"Calamari meatballs?"

"Just in the center," says Paolo.

Dan asks, "Can we also order a black pasta and a large fra diavolo please?"

"You got it, hon'."

"I'm ahh so happy to eat bread again, honey...more vino, per favore." Francesca dips her crust into the red gravy and sips her wine. "Yes, I understand what you are saying. And now when I teach my students, I let the energy flow through me so that they can ahh develop."

"That's exactly right; we are all just clusters of energy. However, for you not to become energy depleted, you also need a continued source of inspiration. And he's sitting right there with gravy all over his face." Paolo belts out a deep laugh in between bites. He wipes the red stains across his thick lips with a paper napkin. Dan gives him two big pats on the shoulder.

"How is Taylor anyway?"

"She's ahh good. Her boyfriend seems nice enough, but I don't talk much ahh with her about these things. It's ahh weird, for Paolo and I...not having you two together. We have all been through so much. Remember when the four of us went to Roma?"

"How could I forget? It was such a wonderful time. So much limoncello! So, when was the last time you two were home?"

"Last ahh August. We spent a month. We plan on going back over winter break. I want ahh to spend more time with my parents you know...they are getting older," says Paolo.

"Well, you give your mamma a big kiss from me, and tell her I still dream of her meatballs." They grin as they reflect on how many meatballs Dan had eaten when they guided him through Rome the last time he visited."

"You know, ahh Dan, the purpose part of our discussion is so important. It reminds me a lot of Victor Frankl's work...huh?"

"Exactly, Paolo. It's purpose that draws energy into our vessels. I do want to say though, that the idea of a vessel may not be the best imagery. I am struggling with this, as I don't want to portray us as separate identities. You know, like Alan Watts teaches."

"Squid ink pasta."

"Just here, we are going to share." The waitress sets the pan on the corner of the table, and Francesca scoops the black, rich noodles into each of their plates. A few minutes later, the fra diavolo arrives, and Francesca repeats the allotment.

"Mmm...delizioso."

"I'll say. This is amazing. Better than ever...mangiare."

They soon finish the fra diavolo and a third bottle of wine. Their conversation is flowing smoothly—this time on how Paolo likes working for BU. Their connection is as it used to be—when they went out as couples, minus one.

"Can I get you anything else?"

They shake their heads. "Guys, I am beyond stuffed."

"We are too."

"Check, please." Dan extends his palm. The waitress wipes her hands on her apron, and she gives him a small piece of paper scribbled with blue ink.

"Oh, Dan... please, let us ahh pay."

"No way. This is on me. Having dinner with you two

was such a pleasure. It means so much to reconnect." Francesca touches Dan's arm.

In an appreciative voice, Paolo says, "Grazie. No, this was our pleasure. Please ahh, we must then go for after-dinner drinks and some dessert."

"OK. But I'm telling you, I don't have much room. Look at this swollen, pasta belly." Dan rubs his two hands over his extended waist. "I might have to loosen my belt buckle."

"Ha, ha. Us too. Let's get some air," says Francesca.

They walk out together onto the congestion of Hanover and decide on cannoli and cappuccinos across the street at Franco's Café. An old man smoking a thick cigar near the doorway fills the air with a syrupy, perfumed cloud. Francesca coughs as she enters, but Paolo and Dan enjoy the aroma.

They find an open table toward the back of the first floor, where a tall server in tight jeans and a white T-shirt greets them. "Paolo, Francesca...my favorite couple, how are ya? Don't you want to sit in the special space downstairs?"

"Come stai amico mio?" They hug and kiss. "No this is fine, Tony. We just ate across the street. Came in for some sweets," says Paolo.

"Everything good at school? I feel like I haven't seen ya in weeks."

"That's because you weren't in church last Sunday," scolds Francesca.

"I know, I was a little under the weathaa, if ya know what I mean." He waves his arm up and down like a pigeon wing.

"This is our friend ahh...Dan."

"Good to meet you, Dan." They shake. "Hey, this guy's

gotta grip." Tony pretends to massage his hand after separating. "Let me get some of the fresh cannoli; we just made 'em. Be right back." Tony saunters off with a cocky stride.

"Seems like a good guy."

"Oh yes. He's an important person to know. A good friend ahh too," says Paolo.

A few minutes later, three guys sit at a nearby table and cloud the air with Drakkar. All are sporting black, long-sleeved shirts with the top three buttons open to their orange chests. The tallest is wearing a red Armani sport jacket. His hair is shiny and meticulously slicked back across his elongated head. Assuming their seats, the men nod respectfully at Paolo, who returns the gesture. Francesca leans over to Paolo and whispers something in his ear. He pretends to ignore her words.

Dan says, "Paolo, we haven't had a chance to talk about your work. What have you been writing about lately?"

"Nothing as exciting as ahh your model."

"Come on. Don't be humble. You're always ahead of the pack."

"Yes, honey, tell ahh Dan, about the book you are working on."

"Book?"

"Yes. I have been writing about post-modernism philosophy in politics ahh. I have been referencing a lot of Foucault's theory of individual oppression by modern political systems."

"That sounds so interesting. Everything comes down to power, doesn't it?"

"You are right on that ahh. Modern political institutions are causing all of our vessels to shrink, but the rate ahh of that decline is so steep ahh in the marginalized." Paolo gestures a downward spiraling motion in the air.

"I can't wait to read it."

"I will send you some draft chapters, my friend. I would like to get your feedback."

"Our politicians absolutely disgust me...same players over and over again...pushing their agendas for their own benefit...just like Rimrodder."

"It's ahh even worse in Italia. Everything is controlled by the..." Paolo catches himself, then leans over and whispers, "Mafia."

In the meantime, Tony returns with three cannoli, cappuccinos, and Sambuca's. He also brings over three medium-sized cartons of pastries. "A little something for the AM, huh? I'm gonna go home a little early tonight. I gotta date." He gestures with his head toward the cash register. It's one of the college girls from across the street. He winks.

Paolo says, "God bless, my friend. Grazie. Will we see you after mass?"

"Yeah, if I skip church tomorrow, Momma will be after me. See you then." Tony leans over and kisses Paolo and Francesca. He gives Dan a partial hug. "Hope to see ya again."

"Yes, good meeting you too, Tony."

Before he heads out, Tony stops at the next table and has a brief discussion in Italian with the three men. They get up and follow him out.

"You like your cannolo, honey?" Paolo lovingly admires Francesca who has a swipe of powdered sugar on her lip.

"I will need to dance for eight hours on Monday. Too much food," she says.

Dan follows, "You don't have to worry. You still have a perfect ballerina figure."

Francesca indeterminately raises her eyebrows and smiles.

Dan holds up his glass. "Down the hatch guys. Mmm...I love Sambuca." He smacks his lips at the warm licorice.

Soon the sugar and alcohol go to work. Francesca rests her head on Paolo's big shoulder, and her eyes close as he strokes her neck. Dan is also fighting to stay awake and breaks his food coma after looking at his watch. "Holy cow, I need to be on my way. Let me catch this last train. I don't know why the T shuts down so early." He takes the last sips of his cappuccino. "This was so wonderful. Thank you both. Buonanotte."

They hug before separating. Dan heads back to the T carrying his pastries. Although he has a full belly, being with Paolo and Francesca leaves him with an insatiable craving. He knows he must see HER again. Monday will be his day.

~~~

Zach

A lobster boat engine causes me to wake at 10 AM. I can't believe how great I slept. I'm feelin' excited about havin' coffee with Megan.

After showerin' and shavin', I anxiously drive to town, where I meet her at the same bench from yesterday. She's lookin' over the harbor when I get there.

"Good morning. Sorry...if I'm late."

"Oh, you're not late. My parents didn't need my help this morning, so I thought I would get here a little early
~~~

and read. I like to look over the harbor when it's quiet like this." She studies me closely and says, "You look different from yesterday."

"Yeah, a showaa can do great things."

"You clean up well," she says with a partial wink.

I blush. "Thanks, I do what I can." I study her for a few seconds. She doesn't feel like a stranger. "So, how 'bout some coffee?"

"Let's do it."

She rises from the bench, and we walk toward a small café just up Main. It's got a green and yellow awning, with Scilles Café outlined in bold, white letters. As soon as we enter, an older lady tendin' the counter stops her routine and offers a warm greetin'. "How are you, Uni?"

"Oh, I'm fine, Mrs. Scilles. How are you?"

"How's your mother and father? I haven't seen them in weeks. Are they well?"

"Yes, they are fine. They have just been crazy busy with the B & B, though."

"Yeah, we sure have gotten the tourists this season. Well, you tell them I send them my love. Now, tell me... who is this handsome gentleman?"

"This is my friend, Zach."

"Marilyn Scilles. Pleasure to meet you."

"My pleasaar, Mrs. Scilles."

"Oh, please call me Marilyn, you know like the movie star." She pretends to fluff her hair. "So, what are you kids having today?"

Megan says, "How about two Green Mountain lattes, Mrs. Scilles?" She looks my way and asks, "Is that OK for you?"

"Perfect," I say.

"You got 'em hon; they'll be out in a minute. Why don't you two go find a seat, and I'll bring them over."

We move to a table near the front window and sit on mismatched wooden chairs softened with yellow cushions clad with flower prints. Our nook smells of pancake syrup, coffee, and bacon. As we settle into our seats, Megan asks me how I became interested in painting.

"I pretty much started in high school. I was kind of a troubled kid but was always good at drawin'. My aart teacher saw some talent and offaaed to give me some lessons aafter school. And heaa I am."

She watches me closely while I talk. "I don't know why, but you look so familiar to me."

Christ, I hope she doesn't recognize me from the news.

"Yeah, a lot of people tell me that. I think I just have a familiaa face."

"I just can't place you." She gets distracted when Mrs. Scilles brings the lattes over. She wipes the table down and sets the cups in front of us. "Just let me know if you kids want anything to eat."

"We will. Thank you." It seems like the perfect time to change the topic. "Why does Mrs. Scilles call you Uni?"

"Well, that's short for my middle name—Unity."

"Huh, I like that name."

She bats her eyes. "Thanks. I guess it's unique."

"So, what did you study in school...UNI?"

After a milky sip of her latte, "I was a pre-med major. But I changed my mind about med school during junior year...after I shadowed a few doctors."

"Why?"

She wipes a line of foam from her top lip with a folded napkin. "Well, it seemed too much like a business. The doctors couldn't spend much time with their patients because the healthcare system pressured them into scheduling a new one every ten minutes. In some cases, I wasn't even sure the doctors knew their patients' names. It wasn't what I thought of when I hoped to study medicine. I just wanted to help people without the business element. Isn't that the Lord's greatest message, to simply help people?"

If she only knew who she was askin'.

"Well, anyway, I moved back in with my parents after college, and I have been working on my master's degree in education."

"Well, that sounds very cool."

"Yeah, I really like it. I want to teach science, even though I believe it's only a snapshot of it all...the cosmos and everything."

"Where do you want to teach?"

"I'm not sure. I know God has a plan for me, but I just don't know what it is yet. For now, I'm happy to live with my parents until I figure it all out." We both take another sip of our lattes. "So, enough about me. Let's talk about you."

"What would you like to know?"

"For starters, what are your religious beliefs? You kind of avoided the question yesterday."

I knew this was coming. "Well, like I said, I don't have any set beliefs."

"Come on, we all believe in something," she says.

After a long pause, "Yeah, I guess. Well, for me, I don't really think of God as a person. It's more like, I don't know...the composition of things...the nature. Like Picaasso in the sky."

"That's such a nice way to think of it. It sounds like Spinoza. What about heaven and the afterlife, do you think this life on earth is all we have?"

Who the F...k is Spinoza?

"I really don't know. I'm having enough difficulty dealin' wit' the here and now. I haven't moved to a place where I can think about what haappens when I die. Simple thoughts for a simple guy, I guess."

"You're not simple."

"Thanks. You know, I really like talking with you, Megaan...I mean, Uni. I haven't felt comfortable like this..."

She cuts me off. "I like talking with you too. You're kind of a mystery—dark and existential."

"How about you? What are your thoughts on an aftaalife?"

"I believe we are made in God's image, and if God is eternal, then we have to be as well."

I'm not sure how to respond, so I don't say anythin'. I inventory her face and think I would need yellow ochre to capture her earthiness, with lemon yellow mixed with red cadmium and a dab of white to highlight her spirituality. I will paint 'er. I got 'er memorized.

"Here's a random question, what are your favorite smells?"

"Huh? That's some question. I don't know. I've nevaa really thought about it," I say.

"Come on..."

I scratch my head. "OK, I guess I like the smell of oil paints. They gotta rich, satisfyin' smell...especially when they're dryin'. I like the smell of oranges too. Actually all citrus. What about you?"

"Well, it's a tie between freshly cut grass and wood

burning in a fireplace."

"Oh, they're good ones. I would list those too."

"See, we have a lot in common." She softly punches me in the arm.

"I guess we do."

"So, when are you going out to paint again?"

"Huh? Well, I was plannin' on goin' out tonight. I wanna' get up to Camden Hills to do a sunset. Do ya think you might like to go with me?"

"I would love to, but won't I be distracting? I wouldn't want to interfere with your work."

"No, it would be great to go there with you." I can't conceal the happy tone in my voice.

"Awesome, I'd love to watch you create."

We slurp up the last drops of our lattes and things get kinda quiet.

Should I tell 'er about my 'psychiatric journey' like Pergo sometimes puts it. I don't wanna freak her out. I'm surprised she even wants to hang out with me given I'm so far away from her deep-seeded religious beliefs. I wanna kiss 'er. God, she's gorgeous.

We get up and say goodbye to Mrs. Scilles, who's frying bacon and eggs on the greasy grill top.

"See you kids, have a wonderful day. Nice meeting you, Zach."

"You too, Mrs. Scilles."

A light wind hits us when we get outside. In this perfect morning, I feel a sense of gratitude. "Hey, what do ya want to do?"

She grabs my hand and starts to skip in a circle. "Do you like books?"

"I don't read much anymore, why?"

"Well, there's this wonderful bookstore up the street. Would you like to go? It's one of my favorite places in this town."

"Sure, that sounds...ummm...interestin'."

We walk up a slight hill and stop to look in the windows of a few shops before coming across a red brick building with a small white sign posted in the window—**Used Books Upstairs**. One of the double doors is propped open with an old encyclopedia. "Here it is," she says, pulling me in. We climb the squeaky stairs in perfect rhythm up to the third floor, where we are greeted by a mildew-like smell. It causes both of us to cough.

The room is wicked warm and dimly lit. Behind the desk sits a tall, skinny guy readin' *Siddhartha* under a small lamp. He's squintin' through round-rimmed glasses pushed to the front of his nose. He sets the book down as we enter, and without moving from his relaxed position, he says, "Greetings, fellow humans. Oh, Megan, it's you. How are things?"

"I'm good, Jerry. Life treating you well?"

"It's far out. Very far out. Nice day, huh?"

"That it is."

"Well, feel free to look around. You know where everything is in this little slice of the universe."

"Yes, I do. Thank you."

We start to explore. The books are arranged by topic across two big rooms. Titles are stacked from the floor to the ceilin'. For a little store, this place houses almost anythin' you could imagine. The dude's got classics, poetry, biographies, modern fiction, and philosophy—a perfect petri dish for mental microbe growth. Me an' Megan separate for a few minutes to look around. When I meet back up with her, she's holdin' *Catcher in the Rye*. She gingerly shuffles the pages like a deck of cards before setting it back on the stack. "I love that book," she says.

At least she likes crazy.

"Yeah, that's a good one," I say.

We start to look through some of the standards—Hemingway, London, Steinbeck, Lee, and Melville. I tell 'er that Steinbeck was my favorite back in high school.

"Why?"

"Because he was anti-establishment. He didn't like the bullshit of it all."

She agrees before becomin' distracted with another rack of books on religion. Like a sprinter, she darts over and starts perusin' through a Catholic encyclopedia. I reluctantly follow. She starts skim-readin' somethin' on Thomas Aquinas, and I start to get itchy. I let 'er go for a few minutes before I interrupt. "Hey, I should go back to the cabin to pick up my geaa. Don't want to miss the sunset."

"Sounds like a good idea. Just let me check the psychology books for a second. I want to get my mom this book about human relationships that we read in psych class last year. I don't remember the author, but it was a pretty cool read. It covered a lot about energy sharing in relationships. My mom and I are so often at each other's throats. Maybe we could use it to help us communicate."

We go over to the psychology area and look through the tall stacks. We don't find anythin' that resembles the book she's describin'. We agree to come back another time to look more closely. After sayin' goodbye to Jerry, I ask, "So, where do you want to meet lataa?"

"How about in front of Scilles, in like...two hours?"

"Great." I give her a thumbs up.

As we part, I have a sense of excitement in my heart. I can't wait to get my stuff and meet back up wit' 'er.

***

When I return to the cabin, I toss my paints, clean-up rags, and canvases in the back seat. I splash some cold water on my face and hair and take a few minutes to comb out some of my brown, kinky curls. I guess I want to look good, even though I can't do anythin' about the birthmark on my neck, a caramel-colored, three-inch, Z-shaped stain that almost looks like a tattoo. Shit, I hate that thing. Megan's definitely seen it, but I guess it hasn't bothered 'er. Like Pergo says, 'learn to accept things that are out of your control.'

I go outside and take a few minutes to look over the inlet. Children on the beach are picking pieces of beach glass. The glare from the glass shines back toward my eyes like tiny lasers. I sit for a while and look at the water before gettin' back in the truck. I turn on the radio and after hittin' fuzz along most of the dial, finally tune in *Color Blind.* I love the Crows and turn it louder while singin' along. Megan is just arrivin' as I pull up. She smiles and waves before openin' the door. In a happy voice, "Perfect timing. Nice truck."

"Thanks. I've had it a few yeaas. It's not easy to paark in the city, but it's a great way to traansport all my stuff."

"Plus, it makes you look rugged," she says sarcastically as she settles into her seat.

I smile and look at her with a quick glance before following with an even longer look of appreciation. She changed her clothes and untied her hair from the ponytail she'd worn earlier. Her black locks shimmer as they fall over her shoulders and light blue tank. As we drive northward, she fades in and out with the shadows cast by the passin' trees. The incoming breeze swirlin' through the passenger window pushes her hair around, and she continually keeps it out of her face by swiping it back with a well-rehearsed maneuver of her wrist—fingers stiff and contorted like a comb.

"I don't remembaa how much furthaa to the paark?"

"Oh, just a few miles. It'll be up here on the left." She points.

A large brown wooden sign marks the entrance. A friendly older guy with sun freckles all over his face meets us at the gatehouse. He accepts the entrance fee and opens the gate for us. We drive up a steep, curvy road to the highest lookout point. When we get up there, the freshness of Maine fills our lungs. We cast out our arms like birds intendin' on flight.

After a few minutes of gazin' at the landscape, we decide that a harbor scene, lookin' down from the mountain would be perfect. I set up the easel and lay out my palette—warm colors on the left, cool to the right. Megan sits on a huge, pale-reddish rock with metallic speckles. She watches me fall into the sketch. I block in the big shadows cast by the sunset and know I need to work fast in the en plein air spirit. These types of paintings are about capturin' the moment—they are visceral. This takes on even more significance with all that I'm feelin'.

Megan looks over the water as I cut in the general shapes. I add some imprecise lines as placeholders for the rocky overlook. She says, "I really think only a grand designer could have put such perfection together." I don't respond and just keep on paintin'. She respects my silence.

I lay down a few orange strokes in the sky and step back from it. Things are quiet, except for the distant humming of people talking against the turbulent wind. I continue to work, some dabs of blue in the rocks, big viridian strokes across the water, a hit of crimson in the sky. Occasionally, I look over at 'er. She's takin' in the same scenery that she is organically part of. I realize I'm fallin' for 'er—hook, line, and sinker. She's right, only a grand designer could have put such perfection together. Since I'm pretty much finished and the light starts to dwindle, I suggest we pack up. She gets up from the rock and walks over to me. She stands close, but stays behind, peekin' over my shoulder. Her hand brushes against my neck. "Wow, I love the gentle, fluid sense of your style," she says.

Her words mean a lot. I feel it building. THERE IS HEAT. Without hesitation, I turn around and pull her in. It's a blur. We kiss. Yeah, quick, but still lip-to-lip. *Oh no, what did I just...?*

She lifts her hand and calmly caresses my face. Our lips meet again, this time—longer. We hold each other and the sun sets. None of it seems real. Here we are, two people, practically strangers, becoming one giant shadow on the top of some mountain in the middle of nowhere. It's like some greetin' card or somethin'. When we pull away, I notice a spot of white paint on her shoulder. When I try to wipe it, she pulls back. "Maybe I'll just keep it there as a reminder." I absorb the feelin' like a dry sponge, thirsty for so long, swellin' with the transformed freedom I'm feelin'...in this place, with this person.

~~~
~~~

Dan

When he enters the gallery in the late morning, Dan is wearing his favorite tan sweater and a comfortable pair of jeans. His hair is immaculately combed back, like the guys from the café. This time he predicted her schedule correctly. She is sitting behind the escritoire when he steps through the doorway. He feels the blood rush to his face when he sees her. Chiara seems slightly taken aback when she realizes it's Dan. She rises from her seat and meets him halfway with a warm smile, "Welcome back, Professor." She offers her hand. "My name is Chiara." She doesn't want to pretend that she doesn't know who he is.

Dan takes her lead, reaches out his own hand, and in a suspended manner says, "Please, it's Dan." He cherishes the touch of her delicate fingers and the reciprocal nature of her handshake. Her nails are polished in a subtle pink. She smells like lavender. "I was surprised to see you at BU. Are you a philosophy major?"

Tucking her hair behind her ears, "Yes, I'm doing my master's. In philosophy."

"What a coincidence. That's what I..."

"I know, right? I enjoyed your lecture the other day. You are a great speaker. I also like how you handled Dr. Rimrodder. He's such a bully."

"Thanks. I do better when I don't have cream cheese smeared all over my face."

"Ha, ha. I'm sure I'm the only one who noticed that."

"Yeah, I hope so. So, what did you think of my vessel model? I'm still not sure if I'm going down a rabbit hole with the concept. I hope you don't mind me coming in here and putting you on the spot."

"No, not at all. I think you're on to something very

interesting. Since your presentation, I've been giving it a lot of thought as it relates to my own life." The phone rings. "Excuse me, I'll be right back." She handles the call quickly and comes back over. "So, can I help you with something today?" Her directness is intimidating. He takes a deep breath and just comes out with it, "Well, I...I actually came to...see you."

Her eyes widen. She asks, "Not to see the art?"

"I am here to see the art, but I'm already talking to the masterpiece." She snickers at his weak game. "I'm sorry, it's just that you made such an impression on me the other day. I just wanted to...I don't know..."

"It's OK. I was hoping you would stop in again. Was it me that you were referring to in the presentation?"

"And then, I saw you in cla..." When he realizes what she just said, he changes his tone. "That obvious, huh? Well, in that case, I'll start stopping in every day." They chuckle. "So, how long have you worked here?"

"Oh, part-time for about a year. I started when I moved from Saint Luis Obispo."

"A California girl, huh?"

"For sure. Can't you tell by my Valley girl accent?" They laugh again. "My dad's an artist. He did the painting you were looking at the other day." They walk over and study it together.

"I'm the baby in the painting and that's my mother. My father knows the gallery owner. That's how I found this job."

"You were so beauti...I mean, so cute...when you were a baby."

"Thanks. You're not going to ask me what happened... since then...are you?"

"Ha, ha. You're funny," he says. She blushes.

Another customer comes in. "Well, I know you have to get back to work. Maybe we can go out for dinner or something sometime. You know, we could talk about philosophy."

She responds, "That sounds really nice. I would enjoy that very much." She scribbles her address and phone number on a slip of paper. He appreciates how easy she makes it.

When he reaches for it, she notices that his hand is swollen. "Hey, what did you do?"

"Oh, I bumped it moving some...furniture." He hides his blue knuckles in his pocket. "So, how's Thursday...say seven?"

"That sounds great. Just buzz me from the foyer when you get to my apartment."

"Will do. See you then." He strides out after they lock eyes for few seconds.

~~~

Zach

It's quiet when we get back in the truck. We hold hands goin' down the mountain, my right sandwiched between both of hers and restin' on her leg.

"Hey, I'm starvin'. How about some dinnaa?"

"Me too. There's a nice café not far from here. Fresh seafood and Americana cuisine. It's kind of romantic, too."

"That sounds good."

"Make the next left. It's up here." She nods at the sign.

"It looks nice. Lotsa caars."

"Yeah, it's pretty popular. Especially on weekends. We
~~~

always recommend this place to our B & B guests."

We get out and walk over a crunchy shell pathway to the entrance. The inside is lined with coarse stone and exposed brick. There are large paintings of schooners on each wall and a big fireplace near the bar. We find a quiet table in the far corner, and we order two glasses of rosé after takin' turns washin' up in the bathroom. Our private recess is lit with a small candle flickerin' in a Mason jar.

"I can't tell you how much I enjoyed today, Megaan. You're aawesome."

She studies me and reaches for my hand. Her fingernails are short but well-manicured in dark, chocolate brown. "You're pretty special yourself."

We read over the menu.

"The shrimp scampi looks good," she says.

"It sure does. I love shrimp."

"Me too, especially when they're fresh. I think that's what I'm going to order. I've had it here before. I remember enjoying it."

"I'm goin' with the lobstaa salad. You eat oystaas? We can split some of those if ya do."

"You're my kind of dining partner," she says.

"I aim to please."

After we place our order with some clueless high school girl, I ask her, "So what else did you do in college? Were you part of any clubs or anythin'?"

She thinks for a moment. "Yes, I belonged to a few clubs, but I spent most of my first two years doing modeling. At first, it was cool, and the money was great, but the other girls were totally messed up. So many were anorexic and wild. Like they say, sex, drugs, and rock-n-roll. So, I found myself starting to miss class and growing totally out of balance. I was partying way too much. Then I got involved with this boy, which ended in a devastating split. I felt like I was in a big vacuum. The whole experience still hurts when I actually stop to think about it. Anyway, I guess that's when I found faith. It has helped me become whole again."

Her honesty is captivating...I can't look away...I'm not sure what this is.

After a sip of wine, I could tell she was ponderin' something. "Hey, are you doin' OK? Maybe this is too..."

She interrupts. "No, I need to tell you something else. There's another guy I started dating in school. I met him at the Newman Center last year and...well, he and I..."

I interject. "Wait, I'm confused. Are you sayin' you gotta boyfriend?"

"Yes, kind of. Nolan is finishing school this year. He's still in Philly, and I don't get to see him much...so well, I'm not sure what the future holds." Her words hurt my head and leave me feeling nauseous. She firmly squeezes my hand. "Maybe I'm looking for something different. I feel connected to you in some strange way. I feel your sense of hurt. I can't help myself from wanting to care for you."

"But, what about Nol...?"

"I'm not sure. I just wanted to tell you so there are no games between us. I just want this to be real. I feel like I can be honest in that way with you...even after just this short time. But Nolan...he expects things of me that I don't think I can... He wants me to move in with him after he graduates, but I'm not sure that's what I want. I don't want to confuse you in my soap opera. I am so sorry. It's just that I really, really like being with you." She leans over the table and climbs my neck with her breath. Her lovely fog moistens my body. She whispers, "I want you to tell stories of me in your paintings. I want to cook for you; I want to decorate your Christmas tree with white and silver. I think I'm falling for this whole broken artist thing you got going on." She again caresses my face with a gentle glide of her hand. I feel a chill when she pulls away. Her spell is mysterious. Minutes go by.

Should I tell 'er about me? No, I can't...She'll think I'm a freak...I am a freak...God, it's so embarrassin'...I can't risk it...She's so honest, and now I'm just goin' to lie...Shit, I feel itchy...

Right before I get the balls to confess my spotted past, her attention shifts across the dining room toward another table. "Don't turn around, but it just upsets me when people eat alone."

Even though I'm not supposed to, I turn to see what's makin' her upset. There's an old guy with an oversized lime-green sport coat eatin' a turkey platter and readin' a magazine. I see him spill some gravy on his shirt, which he cleans up by dabbin' his napkin into a glass of water and then pattin' at it—like Pergo does to my back. I turn back toward Megan and notice a tear in 'er eye.

I say, "Hey, it's OK. At least he's gotta a nice meal. Bein' alone doesn't necessarily make him lonely. I'm sure he's got a family somewhaar." I lightly touch her shoulder while moving my chair closer to hers.

"No, it's not OK. Of all things, turkey shouldn't be eaten without family." She sniffles and wipes her wrist across her nose.

The old fuck bums us out. So, we don't say much for the rest of the dinner. He departs before we do.

He'll be OK. You get used to not havin' anyone to talk with...Nolan will be OK too.

***

Arm-over-arm we get back into the truck and drive back into town. I pull up next to her red Honda Prelude in the empty harbor parking lot and turn off my engine. I reach over and bring her closer. She briefly rests her head on my shoulder before glancing up, leading to a long kiss. When we come apart, she says, "I guess I should go. I don't want my parents to worry."

"Yes...of course...I understand. This...this has been the greatest day, Megaan...thank you. Can I see you tomorrow before I drive back? God, I wish I had more time heaa."

"I sure hope so," she says. "I can't tell you how much I enjoy being with you, Zach. I've never felt this way before." She jumps out of the truck and gets in her car. I wait for her to drive away before I pull out of the lot. I feel like I just ran a marathon. When I get back to the cabin, I collapse on the bed.

~~~

Dan

Dan is both excited and nervous about his date. He rings the buzzer. "Hey, Chiara...it's me, Dan. I'm downstairs."

"OK, great. I'll be right down."

"All right, take your time."

She comes to the door a minute later. She's wearing a long, tan skirt and brown, lace-up boots. Her blonde hair is free flowing across her white blouse.

"Sorry it took me so long to come down. I couldn't find my keys."
~~~

"Not at all. You're right on time. You look nice."

"Thanks."

"Hungry? I was thinking Japanese. There's a new restaurant on Huntington. You interested in trying it? We could walk over."

"That sounds great. I haven't had sushi since I've been here."

"So how have your last couple of days been?"

"Pretty good. Busy with work and all. We're trying to plan a new show. I've been making a bunch of phone calls arranging transportation for the paintings. You would not believe the insurance concerns." They cross the street.

"I can only imagine. Sounds cool. What's the theme?"

"We don't have a title yet, but it's going to focus on southwestern art. There are tons of great painters in places like Santa Fe."

"I know it. I went there a couple of years ago after giving a talk at the University of New Mexico. Drove up from Albuquerque and spent the weekend. I like the energy there."

"Yeah, I think that positive energy is well portrayed in their art, too."

"It sure is. The galleries are great. I remember climbing that hill. The one with all the galleries on it."

"You mean, Canyon Road?"

"I think so...can't remember the name. Here we are. Looks quaint."

They are seated at a small table next to a big fish tank.

Dan asks, "Do you like sake?"

"I do."

"Me too. Let's get some. So, tell me about yourself."

"Well, I used to be a competitive figure skater."

"Really, how competitive?"

"Very...I was ranked in the top five for the US...until I ruined it at nationals. The smallest flaws in execution can cost a skater points, and a few tenths ended my dreams of becoming an Olympian."

"Wow. Top five. That's amazing. Not making the team must be so hard though."

"You have no idea. If I had just skated up to my potential, who knows? Maybe I would have even medaled. I dedicated my whole life to skating and then just failed. I relive it every day." Dan tries to be consoling, but his efforts also seem to fall a few tenths short.

"I'm sorry. I can see this is still really hard for you."

"No, no...I'm sorry. I need to learn to accept it. I don't want to ruin our time together replaying this."

"You're not ruining anything. I like hearing about who you are. No apologies necessary." Dan straightens his chair. "So, what other things do you like to do? Do you have any hobbies?"

"Well, I got into photography when I was a kid. My dad and I would go out in nature—I would take photos while he would paint. It was so fun. That's why I feel lucky being able to work in the gallery. The creativity makes me feel at home."

"That's really neat. Your father sounds like a good guy. Talented, for sure. What about your mom?"

"Well, that's a whole other long story. I don't really know her that well." After a long pause, "I haven't seen her since I was a kid. It's strange, you know. She was a flight attendant...and when I was like six...she left on a trip and...well...she never came back." Dan watches tears form in her eyes.

"What? Oh my G..."

She sniffles. "Yeah, she left us. My dad couldn't stand the ghosts in San Diego, so he moved us up to Saint Luis Obispo under the pretense that he wanted to focus on painting the more mountainous areas of the Pacific coast. We never really discussed what happened. He just told me that my mom had to move to another country for work." Chiara gazes at the catfish skimming the bottom of the fish tank. She continues in a melancholy tone, "I don't mean to get all heavy on you, Dan. I just really have a problem trusting people." She sips her sake.

"I understand. I'm sorry to stir all of this up."

"It's all right, I don't think about it all that often anymore, but when it comes up, I still get emotional."

"I can see why. What a difficult story. You know, I think letting out those feelings is the most important thing a person can do for their psychological health. If you keep it all trapped inside, then you pack that negative energy into your emotional basement. Then it spills over to every other aspect of your life. Thanks for trusting me enough to express it."

Chiara's shoulders take on a more relaxed position. "Have you ever considered counseling instead of academia?"

"Yeah, God knows I could certainly use a counselor in my life. Being one would probably be the cheapest option." They giggle.

"So, tell me about you."

"Well, you already know what I do for a living. Let's see. I grew up in a small town in Pennsylvania and went to college there. And...well, that's where I met my ex-wife."

"Wait, you were married?"

"Yeah, we met at college. I fell hard for her. Then she followed me to New Haven when I started graduate school. We got married there."

"If you don't mind me asking...what's her name?"

"Taylor. We have been split for over two years now. The divorce was just finalized a couple of months ago. Sorry to mention this to you on our first date. It's probably not..."

Teasingly, "Is that what this is, a first date?" She rolls her tongue along the side of her cheek.

"It is for me."

Sarcastically, "Well aren't we a pair, a divorced guy and a failed skater with abandonment issues, together on their first date." Ha, ha, ha...

"Yeah, we are quite a pair. For what it's worth, I feel happy after spending just an hour with you."

"Thanks. I feel like that too. I feel like I can tell you things."

"I'm really glad you said that. I have to tell you, I'm a little embarrassed about our age difference."

"Come on, can't you see I'm an old soul?"

"Yeah, you're a real antique. Look at those cobwebs. When we walked in here, I thought they were going to ask where my niece and I wanted to sit."

"Ha, ha. Uncle Dan. I like it." She takes a long sip of her sake. "So, are you close to Dr. Bettullio? It seems like you two are buddies."

"Well, we met when we were in grad school. We became very close. Did many of our classes together. Then we moved to Boston around the same time. He and his wife, that is. We would go out as couples. His wife is still good friends with Taylor. Anyway, then it all got weird with the divorce, and we kind of grew apart. It's not until just recently, at the talk actually, that we came back together."

"Divorce must be hard."

"It is. It's hard to even describe. It's like, everything you think to be everlasting unravels. You lose a big part of yourself during the process." The server comes over. "More sake?"

"Yes, thank you. So, how about you? Have you had any steady relationships?"

"I've dated, but I've never had a lot of time for boys, with my skating schedule and everything. Plus, as I said, I don't really trust very well." Then in a light-hearted tone, "You must have a bunch of girlfriends, being such a distinguished professor and all."

Dan pretends to slick his hair back. "Yeah, I have a lady in every city."

"Exactly as I suspected." She admires his face. "I know we're not supposed to discuss exes on first dates, but can I ask what happened? I mean with your marriage and everything."

Dan sits further back in his seat and shrugs his shoulders. "I'm still not fully sure. The quick and simple answer is that we grew apart. If you want the long-winded version, I can..."

"I'm happy to listen to whatever you are comfortable sharing."

"OK." He rests his elbows on the table. "Well, I'm just going to put this out there. Taylor thought I had an affair...with this French woman."

Chiara folds her arms over her chest and sits back. Half-kiddingly, "You know, I'm part French, too. Must be something about us." Dan isn't laughing. Apologetically, she says, "Sorry, go on, I don't want to make light of this."

"OK, soooo, I was attending the American Psychological Association meeting in Dallas, and I met this woman... Eva, at the hotel bar. I was sitting there, minding my own business, when she pulls up to the stool next to me. She was very attractive, flaunting everything in a blue sequined dress. We started talking. I mean, it was nice. She was an interesting person and everything...and then we had some champagne...and then more champagne...and three hours later, we were hammered. That's when she asked me to help her to her room. She felt dizzy or something. When we got to her door, I escorted her inside, but only for a second." He makes a one sign with his index finger. "She was so wobbly and everything. Anyway, then I gave her a goodnight kiss on the cheek. I mean, it was more of a courtesy than an advance. In retrospect, maybe it was an act of spontaneity...I don't know. She invited me to stay the night and started taking off her dress. Well...it made it almost impossible to refuse. But I did. Refuse, that is...and that's the truth." Some beads of sweat form on the top of his upper lip. He dabs it with his napkin.

"Well, none of what you did sounds all right, but it still seems extreme to be the cause of a divorce. If you really didn't do anything, what made Taylor think you slept with her?"

"That's the really strange part. I went back to the bar after I got Eva to her room because I had forgotten my credit card. There were a bunch of these Texan business types around the bar asking me, 'How'd it go, y'all?' God, their drawls were so annoying. Anyway, I thought it was peculiar that these fake cowboys were so interested in my business, so I ignored them. After I retrieved my card, I went back up to my room for the night and flew back to Boston the next day. I never said anything to Taylor about any of it. I mean I wasn't proud of my actions, but as I said, nothing happened. Then about two months later, the whole evening reopened when Taylor showed me some photographs that she received in the mail—Eva and I outside of her room, the goodnight kiss, Eva undressing. I tried to explain all of it away, but Taylor wouldn't have it. We fought for weeks...until...she asked me to move out. Then, she got involved with someone else. Hah, there it is. A seventeen-year relationship down the tubes over something that never even happened."

"Why would someone send her those kinds of pictures? Do you have enemies?"

"That's what has been driving me crazy." His face reddens. "I have no idea who would have done such a thing. The envelope obviously didn't have a return address. I'm suspicious of those Texas guys though. I think they had something to do with it. If I only knew, I would make them p..."

"I am sorry you went through that. It sounds terrible." She reaches for his hand.

"Ouch." He reflexively pulls back.

"Oh, sorry. I forgot that's the hand you hurt. Are you all right?"

"Yeah, it's just tender."

"Maybe you should get an X-ray. You think it's broken?"

"No, it's just a bruise. It'll get better. So, Taylor and I have a mutual friend from college—Maggie. I had coffee with her one day after all of this happened, and she told me that she believed my story. She also went on to say that she thought the whole Eva thing was just a symptom of my bigger problems."

"What do you mean?"

"She told me that she thought I have no clue about my own insecurities. She thought my flirtatious escapades were because I was afraid of growing old, and I just needed some reaffirmation that I was still desirable. At first, I felt insulted, but now that I think about it, she was right. Hell, I didn't see all this junk in myself. Maybe I need to go back and repeat that class—some expert I am."

"I guess we're all insecure."

"Maybe. I just feel so stupid about all of this. I think that's why Paolo and his wife avoided me. They were mad at my indiscretions."

"Did you talk this through with Dr. Bettullio?"

"No. We kind of ignored the whole topic. I'm just glad we reconnected. I even had dinner with he and his wife the other night."

"Did you mention me at all?"

"I was going to ask him about you after my talk, but I didn't think it would be wise." Dan rolls his eyes.

"Yeah, maybe it would be weird." Chiara downs her sake. "So, what about your parents and family?"

"Well, both of my parents died years ago."

"Sorry. I'm glad I haven't had to go through that yet. Even though my mom and everything..."

"Yeah, I think the kind of abandonment you've experienced is like death though. They are both such painful events. Love and loss seem to go hand-in-hand. My first involvement with death was with my dog, Ellis. God, I loved that guy."

"What kind of dog was he?"

Dan smiles. "A big golden retriever...with an even bigger heart." He extends his arms.

"Oh, I love big dogs. I wish I got to meet him."

"Yeah, you would have loved him. He was so kind. I still can't get over him, and that was so long ago."

"Do you have any photos?"

"Yeah...I keep a couple at home. When he got sick...with cancer...he had this absent look in his eyes. It's so hard to describe...it was like he was staring out toward the universe. My dad, who died a couple of years later with dementia, had that exact same gaze. They both had brown eyes, and you couldn't tell the difference between them. I often wonder what they saw. Hey, let's change the topic. This is starting to bum me out."

"OK. Hey, I forgot to ask you: Did you hear Rimrodder was assaulted near his house the other night?"

Dan slightly squirms around in his chair. "RR...Really? No, I didn't...I haven't been keeping up with the news. Is he all right?" His voice is high pitched.

"Rumor has it that he's OK. From what I heard, someone came up behind him and hit him in the side of the head. It's weird...no robbery or anything...just assault. He lives in a nice section of Brookline. It's just so uncharacteristic. He probably just fell and made the whole thing up to get sympathy from the students."

"I wouldn't be too surprised if he did."

~~~

Delano

It is a cold day in March. Del stares out of the kitchen window of his parents' small house. He has an absent look
~~~

in his tired eyes. The ugly scene of blackened snow and ice elicits a sense of utter disgust within his core. He knows, the caustic burn will only be relieved when he's able to leave this place and return to the university. The few isolated glimmers of reflected light from the snow appear misplaced in this black hole, for hopeful rays have no right to pass through such a pessimistic prism. This was not what he had imagined for junior year spring break.

The demented, all-consuming one enters, wobbling into the room, with knock-knees and a Parkinsonian shuffle that transports at least two equally annoying, unstable personalities. Number one, the incapable, helpless child was visiting now—sobbing while rubbing his gaseous swollen belly. After a few belches, he sidles up to Del, leans over with an open mouth, and asks in a crippled tone. "Look here, look here, can you see it?"

"See what?"

"Here, here, the water...can't you see it?" He points to a third molar with his long, claw-like fingernails, crookedly positioned on gooseneck rheumatoid-ridden fingers.

"No there's nothing there, what do you want me to do?"

"The watcha-ma-call-it. The water, the czezzy..." He draws out the sentence, in a voice craving attention, maybe even empathy.

Del doesn't have any energy left for empathy. He's exhausted and disgusted. The all-consuming one was up throughout the night, every two and a half hours peeing himself. Yeah, Del changed the diapers and helped him wipe his ass, but empathy—not now—maybe never again.

"Go sit down, there's nothing in your teeth, try to

relax." The words fall out of Del's mouth despite his full realization that OCD never relaxes. He had learned about it in his 300-level neurobiology class last fall.

Again, the mouth opens and the all-consuming one points to his gums, saggy and pink, with glistening hints of whitish plaque. Del tries to look away, tries to ignore it, but the all-consuming one is not to be outdone. He inches closer and flairs his lips out in an oval, monkeyesque expression, "Here, here, the cheloa..."

Del feels his pulse rise. He is experiencing the phenomenon of caregiver stress—a situation when the sick ironically kill the healthy. Del resents his father. He resents his madness, his demands, his neediness, his inability to find words. The dementia, sometimes softened by his medications, was only getting worse. His neurobiology professor explained to the class that OCD often occurs with degenerative neurobiological diseases, but Del knew the all-consuming one to have OCD long before dementia. His modus operandi—always everything just in its place, neat, controlled. Felix Unger had nothing on his father.

To remove himself from the situation, Del walks into the living room and turns on some music. Sometimes music calms his father. Del positions himself on the edge of the couch, and his father follows to the adjacent cushion. Pointing to his glasses, he says, "How about this here?"

"What's on the glasses?" Del's face is tense.

"There's water, some watcha-ma-call-it. What-a-you-call?"

Del hands his father a small piece of tissue paper to wipe the glasses. The task takes a few minutes. When he finishes, his father slides them to the top of his roman nose and studies the room. He seems calm and is soon tapping his foot to the rhythm of some 1940's style orchestra tunes. Del seizes on the quiet and picks up a book he needs to read for school. He has a few exams when he gets back after break, and he figures it could be a good time to get some studying in. Like clockwork, the all-consuming one sees Del is not paying him attention. His mouth is back in Del's face a few seconds later.

Del is boiling and gets mean. "I told you there's nothing in your teeth. Stop bothering me with this." His voice is raised and intimidating.

Enter number two. "Shut up, you. Don't you...I'll put my fist in..."

Now, Del grows even angrier and yells back. "Go ahead and try. We can end your pathetic life right now." Though he's hated number 2 since he was a kid, Del feels like shit with his own short temper and horrible words. He knows there is a genetic element for intermittent explosive disorder, which he thinks his dad also has. He worries about his own personality—no, he hates his own personality, too. It seems that neither of them can help it.

"You! Nobody cares about me...ga-fzedled."

Del doesn't respond. He fights back a tear and stares down at the gold bracelet he wears on his wrist to help him feel focused. The intricate links are supposed to remind him of how the universe is all connected. Seeing things at a higher level with obscure philosophical thoughts somehow brings calmness to Del. Ironically, his father taught him that.

The all-consuming one now starts to shuffle into the kitchen to bother Del's mom, who is drinking coffee at the table. "Time to go now...thank you, honey." Sounds like number 1 has returned.

She asks, "Go where?"

"Time to go to my mother's house. She's expecting me."

"Your mother called and said you should just stay here today."

The all-consuming one never listens. Although his mother has been dead for years, he starts searching for a jacket. He comes across his blue bathrobe and thinks it will suffice. He positions it over his shirt, and secures it with the tie, looking a bit like Hugh Heffner. He fiddles with the locks in the back-entry way, and despite Del's best efforts to keep him inside, steps through the door and hobbles outside. Del knows if he just follows the all-consuming one, he will immediately want to come back inside because of the bitter cold. Twenty steps later, his father is searching for ways to get back in. Del leads him to the door.

Del could see the toll that this disease has taken on his mother. She was now trying to distract her own self, looking at the same blackened snow through the kitchen window. The all-consuming one says "Hey there, sis. Look who I found outside...it's our brother." Neither Del nor his mom offers a correction. Now, the monkey face is back. "What's here...the csemai...the water?"

It's still morning.

The phone rings. His mother picks up and extends the greeting in a false, indifferent tone. "Yeah, whatever," is the standard answer to a series of questions that Del assumes is coming from a friend. Del does not know the nature of the questions, but his mother is very terse with each response. Finally, she says something substantial, something significant: "I dread mornings—I hate waking up." It's the first authentic thing Del has heard from his mother's mouth in weeks. He knows she is under incredible pressure and that the all-consuming one has nearly broken her. She has become just a depressed fragment of her former, happy self.

The all-consuming one is now trying to spit out of the kitchen window. "No, let's go into the bathroom, OK?"

"All right," he says. Del's noticed that when his father was unoccupied, he was constantly ridding himself of three out of the four Greek humors—black bile, yellow bile, and phlegm. Del thought the hours his father spent in the bathroom purging his insides was his attempt to exorcise his mental demons. One demon removed with each expulsion of mucus or shit.

A few minutes later, things calm after his father finishes in the bathroom with his most important of rituals—the hand wash. The ceremony is performed about thirty times a day, where he dries between each finger until they squeak. Today is no different, and after setting the towel back on the holder, he asks Del, "Hi there, buddy...can you tell me if there's something in my teeth?"

~~~

Dan

"I'm totally excited, I love acoustic music," says Chiara.

"Yeah, me too. Chelsea is great. I can't wait for you to hear her."

"I like the Red Line too. Much better than the Green. I mean, going over the bridge is actually fun."

"Yeah. See the sailboats? We should do that sometime," Dan suggests.

"Are you asking me out for another date?"
~~~

"You can think of it as a standing invitation."

She wraps her arm under his. "OK, but only if I get to steer the boat."

"You got it, captain." Dan salutes.

The train creaks to a squeaky stop at Davis square. Dan and Chiara exit the platform and walk a few blocks to the venue. A couple of guys with long, greasy hair are standing outside smoking cigarettes, while their friend in a tie-dye T shirt collects change in a tambourine. A stern-faced guy at the door checks their IDs, studying Chiara's without barely looking at Dan's. He signals for them to go in.

"He studied yours so closely. He must think you're seventeen."

"That's because of my height. Everyone thinks I'm younger because I'm a little vertically challenged."

"Good things come in small packages." He pats the top of her head.

"That's what my dad always tells me."

"Hey, Doc." Dan looks through the hazy, smoke-filled club and sees Chelsea rushing over.

"Hey there, Chelsea." They hug.

"I'm so glad you could come."

"I wouldn't miss it for the world. Chelsea, I would like to introduce you to Chiara."

"Hi, Chelsea. Dan has told me so many great things about you."

"Nice to meet you, Chiara. So...Doc, you didn't tell me you were bringing a companion." Chelsea sticks her elbow in Dan's gut for a few fake blows.

"I didn't know either. I just met this girl on the T."

"Ha, ha."

"So, what time do you go on?"

"In like 15 minutes. Why don't you find a table? They serve all kinds of creative cocktails here."

"Perfect. Let's go up near the stage. Hey, Chelsea, break a leg." She reciprocates with a thumbs up.

"I'll be right back; I have to head to the ladies' room," says Chiara.

"OK, I'll order us a couple of beers."

Dan goes to the bar and orders two beers before meeting Chiara back at the table. She's a little frazzled when she comes out. "You wouldn't believe how many girls were snorting coke in the bathroom. You see that girl dressed like Madonna over there? She must have done three lines just when I was washing my hands."

"I know, it's really a problem. We have it going on all over the college."

"I have never done a drug in my life. Have you?"

"If pot counts, then yes. When I was a kid mushrooms and acid were the big things. Everyone was after spiritual enlightenment, Timothy Leary, and all. I stayed away from that stuff though. Now everyone seems to want stimulants. It's a strange generation."

"Hey watch it, grandpa."

Dan leans over the table and brushes against Chiara's shoulder. He toasts, "To the most interesting lady." They sip their beers. The lights dim and a spotlight focuses on Chelsea tuning her guitar before breaking into the first set—a classic arrangement of Carol King and Joni Mitchell. The audience immediately connects and applauds each song with great appreciation. She then goes off script with a few silky renditions of Cat Stevens. The applause grows even louder. "Thank you all, one more before I take a short break." She does *Dog and Butterfly*.

Chiara leans over and whispers, "I love butterflies...I can't believe how good she is."

"I know...I just love listening to her. She has such a great soul; she carries it over to her schoolwork too. She's one of my favorite students ever."

Chelsea comes over to the table. "So, what did you guys think of the first set?"

"Chelsea, you are unbelievable. You made me cry with *Tapestry.*"

"Thanks, Chiara. That song means a lot to me. I really relate to it. Hey Doc, I know you like Heart; I thought you'd like that last one."

"It gives me such vivid memories of when I was a boy. My dog would always chase butterflies. That was such a phenomenal set." He claps. "Bravo, bravo."

"I remember you telling us about that," says Chelsea. "By the way, how's your writing coming along?" She pulls up a chair while Dan flags down the server to order more beers.

"OK, I guess. I made a few edits from our conversation with Noah and Jason."

"That's good. Let me know if you want me to read over any of the new material." She repositions herself to face Chiara. "So, Chiara...how about you...what do you do?"

"Right now, I'm a grad student at BU."

"Cool. What are you studying?"

"Philosophy."

"Oh, so that's how you know Doc..."

"Sort of..."

"Well, he's the best mentor ever." They both glance at him while he is distracted taking in the rest of the room. "Do you have a thesis topic?"

"Yes, I just started it. I'm writing on guilt."

"Awesome, that's a great topic. How are you approaching it? Seems abstract."

"I'm trying to correlate it to the wise, old man archetype. You know, it's like we all have this idea that another being is watching over us—judging us." She looks up at the stage lights. "When we don't live up to certain standards, we feel as if we let the wise, old man down and that makes us feel guilty."

"That's for sure," says Dan rejoining the conversation.

"Yeah." She shrugs her shoulders. "I've been working hard on trying to put it all together."

"Well, it sounds like a great topic," says Chelsea before being signaled by the manager to start the next set. "Sorry, I have to get back to the stage. Hopefully, we will get to talk more sometime." Chelsea chugs her beer.

"I hope so," says Chiara.

Dan calls out, "Chelsea, we may head back downtown before your next break. I'll see you tomorrow if we don't catch up later. OK? You were simply great tonight. Thanks for such a nice evening."

"Thank you for coming, Doc...and thanks for the beer too. Great meeting you, Chiara."

Chiara stands and hugs Chelsea goodnight. Dan likes that they've already bonded. She and Dan hang around while Chelsea starts the second set, consisting mostly of originals. The crowd quiets and becomes absorbed in her powerful lyrics.

"Hey, you want to go get a snack? I'm hungry."

"Yeah, the beer gave me the munchies," she says.

"Let's just do a taxi; I don't want to wait for the T again. How's pizza? I have just the place," he says.

"Yum."

A few minutes later, a cab drops them off in the North End. Fortunately, there isn't a line for *Regina's,* and they are able to walk right in and sit at a corner booth. Chiara loves the retro atmosphere. They order a pitcher of beer. "I think your thesis is going to be great. It's such a good topic."

"Thanks. I can't wait for you to read it," she says.

"I can't wait either. You know, I never asked—what got you interested in the topic?"

"The obvious. I feel guilty all the time."

"About what?"

"Like everything. Especially with my dad. I feel like I must have done something to drive my mom away. Then, I feel guilty that I let him down with my performance at nationals. He has been such a powerful influence on me. I guess that's the old, wise man part. I just cannot shake my feelings over it. It's terrible." She crosses her legs. "Do you feel guilty over anything?"

"Yeah, a million things."

"Like what?"

"Hell, I feel like I let my parents down when they were sick. I feel guilty over letting Taylor down. I was too controlling. I feel guilty when I'm short with people." He shakes his head. "God, this is like a confession."

"Say three Hail Marys, young man."

"You do have good wit, Miss Chiara. You ought to be on stage."

"Wait, I know that one...the next stage outta town," they say in unison. "Ha, ha, ha."

The pizza is steaming hot. Dan dumps garlic oil all over his slice. She asks, "Want some pizza with your oil?"

"You have to pour some on. It's awesome." She drizzles some on her slice. "But seriously, what I want to say is you can't feel guilty over your mom; you were just a little girl. You couldn't have had anything to do with it."

"I know, but feelings are feelings. Mmm, this oil is good. This is the best pizza I've ever had."

"I know. This place is a national treasure." He takes a big swig of beer. "You now have me thinking about how guilt fits into my vessel model. Maybe our archetypes are actually little vessels within the whole. They impact our energy too. I can't believe I haven't thought about this before. See you made this wise, old man's night."

"You're pretty witty yourself. It does kind of fit with your model. I have been approaching my thesis more from a religious perspective though. You know, God the wise, old man judging our sins. We feel guilty when we break a commandment or let God down."

He dabs her mouth with his napkin. "Sauce." He puts another two slices on their plates. "That's one of the reasons why Nietzsche was so opposed to formal religion. He thought it induced guilt and neuroses that made people want to deny the world...make them weak...accepting... easy to govern."

"Yeah, I have a few lines about his thoughts in my introduction. I guess the idea that God is always judging us can induce neurosis. But don't you think that faith in something bigger can also provide a sense of security?"

"For sure. I try not to judge people, one way or the other, on their beliefs."

"My dad and I were pretty observant Catholics when I was a kid," she says.

"Hey, be careful, don't burn your mouth. This cheese

is still really hot." Dan blows over the top of his slice before continuing. "Yeah, my family was pretty religious when I was growing up, too. My dad was in the Knights of Columbus and everything. It's weird how people change. How their kids grow up completely different from them. I'm somewhere between agnostic and atheist. I have to say, I remember being happier when I thought someone was looking out for me, though."

"I'll look out for you," she says.

"Nothing would make me happier." They kiss.

"You taste like garlic," she says.

"I thought that was you. Ha, ha. Hey, maybe you can help me with interpreting this weirdo dream. Maybe guilt has something to do with it," he says.

"You remember your dreams?"

"Not always, but this one occurs so often. It always starts with me being in a place like a basement with long hallways. I keep trying to get outside...but instead, I get deeper in these mazes...these labyrinths. Then I always feel like I am late for something. I try to find my way out... but can't. So, I stop and ask random people for directions on how to get out. They always steer me to an elevator, but since I hate elevators, I instead try to find the stairs. Every time I do, I come out lost. I find myself on top of a wide hill that overlooks a city. There are all these tall, silver buildings with glass windows...you know, kind of like the Pru. Somehow, I always sense that the scene is part of BU, on like the west side of campus." He sips from his mug. "Then, when I try to get to where I'm going, I descend these huge stairwells into really dangerous neighborhoods where thugs chase after me. I run for hours. I wake up and never get anywhere. It's such a horrible feeling. Frustrating."

"Sounds like you need a guide. Maybe, I can be your compass." She winks.

~~~

Zach

"I really don't wanna go, Megaan. I feel a little sick thinkin' I might not see you again."

"Well, we are not going to let that happen. How about I come and visit you next weekend."

"You would do that?"

"You bet. All I can say is that these last two days have been a whirlwind of emotion for me. Even though I still need to pray over this, I'm hoping...well, I thank God for sending you to me. I'll call you tomorrow and we will arrange it. OK?"

"Yes, more than OK."

"Be careful driving back."

"I will. See you soon. I'll call ya when I get home."

***

Driving back to Boston, I melt into nothingness—a snowman on a warm day. When I finally get to Southie after battlin' a nasty jam in Chelsea, I pull into my parkin' spot and lug my gear back in. Everythin' seems so weird. It's like I don't even live here anymore. I fall asleep early and dream about 'er.

The next mornin' I feel inspired to paint. So, after I make myself a fried egg and wash it down with some OJ, I walk over to the studio. I add some touch-ups of cobalt
~~~

blue to one of my brownstone paintings and start a sketch of Megan sittin' on a rock at sunset. A couple hours later, I make my way over to Pergo's office, where after arriving a little early, I'm greeted with a hardy hello and a warm smile by Anna. "Hi there, Zach. You look great. So invigorated."

"Thanks. I was up in Maine. Got some rest."

"Sounds so nice. Just take a seat. Dr. Pergo will be ready to see you in a minute."

"OK." I sit in the empty waitin' room and I pick up a magazine that's runnin' a story on a celebrity divorce. I skim the article and start to feel sad for the couple. It must be hard for them to go their separate ways.

A few minutes later, Anna tells me that Pergo's ready. I walk into his office with a sense of confidence. He immediately steps out of his chair, moves around the desk, and puts a hand on each of my shoulders. He steps back and looks me over from head to toe. "You look fantastic. I can't wait to hear all about your trip."

"You're not even going to believe it. I have so much to tell ya."

"Well, go ahead. I'm all ears."

I share my story for forty minutes, describin' everythin' about 'er. He intently listens with a surprised look on his face. When I get to the part about spontaneously kissin' 'er, his frickin' eyes almost pop out of his head.

"I can barely believe this. I knew you were doing well... but opening up like this to another person...holy cow...it really signals great progress. I am so proud of you! How do you feel about it all?"

"I feel sick. She has permeated me. All I do is think about 'er. Leavin' was like...like gettin' the wind knocked out of me. Like I said, she's supposed to visit for a few days this weekend. I really can't wait."

"Well, that's wonderful. Did you say anything about your mental health?"

After a long pause. "I couldn't. I don't want her to think of me that way. I am really afraid of turnin' her off."

"But don't you think she deserves to know your truest self? If you care for this young lady, you have to present an honest portrait."

"I know you're right, but I'm not sure how to tell 'er."

"Maybe I can help you. I think we can do this in a way that is non-confrontational. If she is uncomfortable with your past, we can talk it through. I want her to know, that as an expert in this field, I believe you have grown to handle your condition. Everything I am sensing from you is exceptional. I feel your empathy. I see before me a sensitive young man who is moving beyond his demons. I'm not saying that you are fully healed. I just think that Megan is falling for a great person. She just needs to know the whole of that guy. Why don't the three of us meet when she comes to visit on Saturday? I will bring some coffee and doughnuts, and we can work it all out, informally. I realize it's a big hurdle, but it is the right thing to do. Think about it."

I rub the scruff along my chin. "OK. Thanks, Doc...I'll let you know."

"Tell me more. What else did you do in Maine?"

"I did some paintin', ate a lot of lobstaa, and did some thinkin'."

"Well, it sounds like a fun, productive trip. You deserve to have some quiet reflective time. You've been through a lot. Think of all the progress you've made."

"I know, I'm not even sure who I am anymore." He doesn't respond. He jots down a few notes in my file.

***

Over the next days, Megan and I talk on the phone. I feel impatient. Time's standin' still, like it does when you're a kid on a hot summer afternoon. I need to stay occupied, so I sketch.

~~~

Dan

As their dates exponentially multiplied over the next year, Dan and Chiara became inseparable. They shared their wants, needs, and hopes. They made love. Chiara fully grew to trust Dan, and she started each morning reading the poem he wrote for her after their first date.

Light

You look to the left
Poised downward in thought
Without makeup, without pretense, with humility
Your nose crinkles when you smile

Warm light thaws the wintery glass
  and I look to you for hours...wanting more
Age after beauty
Story after story
~~~

A circle of questions
Brown eyes melting
Lips imagining...

Maybe I am here to tell you
That inspired elegance always wins
And that far beyond a necklace of heavy metal
Your magic gift bonds humanity and makes wilted hearts blossom again

They were both excited about the success of Dan's book. It was now on the NY Times Best Seller List, and Dan was doing readings and speaking engagements all around the country.

Since Chiara thought it time for Dan to meet her father, they planned a small vacation to visit him after a presentation Dan had scheduled in San Francisco. Their agenda was simple; they would visit Napa Valley right after Dan's talk and then drive down and spend a week with her father. In Napa, they had a romantic weekend of mud baths, gourmet foods, and wine.

On their way to Saint Luis Obispo, they stopped for an afternoon at Muir Woods, where they packed a picnic and sat in a shady meadow underneath some giant redwoods.

"The light here is amazing," says Dan. "This place makes my life feel so small; I'm just a couple of concentric circles within those giant trunks. How do they keep on growing when the entire world around them is changing?"

"Why don't you ask one of them?"

He rises from the picnic blanket. "Hey, Mr. Sequoia, how do you keep reaching toward the sky when so many want to cut off your limbs?" He looks back at her, "I think he's ignoring me. Must want to focus his energy on bigger things." He returns to his spot on the blanket after patting the trunk with the palm of his hand.

"Wait, let me get a photo of you next to that tree. I want to remember this picnic." He stands back up, and she snaps the shot.

"This sounds morbid, but I think I would like to be buried here," he says.

"What are you talking about?"

"It's just so peaceful. It seems like the right place to scatter my ashes when I go. They could fertilize these trees, you know, help 'em reach even greater heights... What's the biblical quote? Something like, 'for dust thou art, and unto dust shalt thou return...' I guess that's all the vessel is anyway—dirt."

"Do me a favor and don't die. How would I live without you?"

"Don't you think about that sometimes? I'm so much older than you are. I have to be the one that goes first. Plus, men don't even live as long as women."

"No, I don't...I can't imagine living witho..."

"Stop, stop...I'm just kidding...I feel the same way. Let's promise not to die. Pinky swear."

"I'm serious."

"Nice to meet you, Serious. I'm Dan."

"Come on," she yells.

"Look, we can't worry about the future. We'll just cross that bridge when we get there. OK? Let's just enjoy the time we have now. Lighten up. We're on vacation."

"I just don't like joking about that stuff. Hey, I'm feeling raindrops." She holds her hand out.

"Me too. Look at those clouds. We better get back to the Jeep." They hurriedly pack up their picnic and run back to the parking area. “Man, that came in fast,” says Dan while huffing and puffing. “It’s torrential.”

“I know. How rude to rain on our picnic,” she says.

“We should write a complaint. How should we address it?”

“To Whom It Rain Concern. Ha, ha.” She laughs at her own joke while fixing her hair. “I’m just glad we didn’t get drenched. I hate driving all damp and everything. Hey, let’s take Highway 1, the scenic route.”

“OK, but I’m not sure we will see much in this storm. We’ll give it a try anyway though. I heard it’s beautiful,” he says.

“It is. My father used to drive us on it all the time.”

After an hour on the road, the storm intensifies. When they encounter a random mudslide that renders the route unpassable, they turn around and spend the night in a motel. Chiara calls her father and explains the situation. The next morning, after the system passes over and everything is cleared, they drive to St Louis Obispo in only a light drizzle. They make it in good time and enjoy the gorgeous ocean views on the way.

“We’re here. Make a left at that driveway,” she says.

Dan steers off the road and courses up a steep hill along the narrow, gravel driveway. At the top of the hill, they park a few yards from a solitary stone house overlooking acres of overgrown fields and wildflowers. After opening their doors and slowly exiting, they stretch the stiffness out of their heavy legs. Within seconds of stepping out of the jeep, a tall, lean, gray-haired man with paint-stained jeans and a partially unbuttoned blue and red flannel shirt comes running towards them from the house. He picks Chiara up with his muscular arms and spins her around in fast circles. Chiara kisses her father's two-day-old beard.

"I missed you, sweetheart," he says as he lowers her to the ground.

"I missed you too, Daddy." She has a tear in her eye.

"Daddy, let me introduce you to Dan."

"Welcome, Dan. I'm Levy Dawson, Chiara's father." Levy extends his hand.

"Mr. Dawson, it's a pleasure to meet you." Their words are consummated by a stern, vigorous handshake.

"Please, call me Levy. Come in, come in...you kids make yourself at home after that long trip." The scent of wet earth greets them as they march onto the porch. "I was so concerned about you in this weather. Those mudslides must have been terrible. I'm glad you didn't get hit by them."

"Oh, Daddy, when are you going to stop worrying about me? I'm a grown woman."

"Yes, you are, ma belle princesse, a perfect grown woman. But the answer is, I will worry about you through infinity." Levy breathes her in. To him, Chiara is royalty. His huge blue eyes light up as he studies her. He grabs the travel bags from Dan.

"It's so good to be home, Daddy."

"I couldn't wait. It's been too long." He kisses her again.

As they talk, Dan admires a gigantic impressionistic painting on the center wall of the foyer—a Monarch butterfly—orange, black, and white, and perched on a purple flower.

"Daddy painted that one for my thirteenth birthday."

"Wow. Levy, I can't tell you how much I love your work."

"Thanks. If you want, I can show you some others back in the studio once you get settled in."

"I would enjoy that."

They move further into the living room. The open floor plan is inviting and warm. Dan sits in a big fluffy chair near the fireplace.

Levy asks, "How about a beer? You must be thirsty from that long drive."

"Not at the moment. Thank you, though. I'll just wait for Chiara," who had journeyed upstairs to check out her old bedroom.

"So, I understand you're a professor and an accomplished author."

"Well, I don't know how accomplished. But yes...my most recent book has been doing pretty well."

"It's so good to hear. We sure do need some deep thinkers in this world, especially here in California, where everyone seems to be losing their minds."

"It's like that in Boston, too."

"I would love to read your book sometime."

"I would be honored if you would. I think I have a copy in my bag. If not, I'll mail one to you when I get back home," says Dan.

"That would be great." Levy pauses and rubs his hands over his knees. In a stern, yet inquisitive voice, "Chiara tells me you two are in love."

Dan respects Levy's direct approach. Looking eye-to-eye, "We are. I want you to know I think Chiara is the most special person I have ever met. Being with her has changed my life." Dan reflects on his age and adds, "I know it seems strange that Chiara and I could have a relationship with our age difference, but...well...it just happened."

Levy lets Dan finish speaking. "Well son, I was initially concerned about the age difference, but I can see you make her happy, which is the only thing that really matters to me. I'm glad my little princesse found her prince."

"Hmm, you know what, maybe I will have that beer now," says Dan.

"Good idea."

A few minutes later, Chiara prances down the stairs and finds them both sipping on pale ales. She is holding Cody, one of her old stuffed animals. She nestles up close to her dad on the couch and buries her round head on his shoulder. He wraps his long arm around her. The orange-blue flames from the fireplace crackle and pop. Their shadows dance on the limestone below the pine mantle.

"You know, Dan, Chiara and I used to often sit at this fireplace before her skating competitions. We used to lose ourselves in the flames as a sort of meditative device."

"It is very calming. This is such a great place. It has such a sense of balance."

Chiara smiles at Levy. "Yeah, Daddy is big into Feng Shui. I used to think his preoccupation with it was so weird. I was even embarrassed to bring friends over when I was a kid."

"I remember that," says Levy. He embraces Chiara even more tightly. "Honey, how's school going?"

"It's going pretty well. My thesis is coming along. I hope to graduate on time. Will you be able to come to Boston for graduation, Daddy?"

"I wouldn't miss it for the world. I can't wait. I gotta tell you...it's so good to see you kids. I am just so happy that you're here. Let me fill us up on drinks." As Levy starts to make his way into the kitchen, he tells Chiara to show

Dan around the house.

When they are alone, "So, what do you think of him?"

"He's such a great guy. You are so lucky to have each other." They stand and kiss, only to separate like sixth graders playing spin the bottle when Levy returns from the kitchen carrying a tray full of hors d'oeuvres and three glasses of a local sauvignon blanc. He toasts, "To Chiara and Dan." They tap their glasses and Chiara gives both of her men huge hugs. Dan enjoys the complex notes of vanilla and oak, sliding his tongue along his upper lip. As Chiara and Levy catch up, he makes his way to the fire and starts poking at the coals to spark the dwindling embers. After igniting a few small flames, he sets the fire prod to the side. They talk the afternoon away.

***

"Hey let's eat," says Levy. "I'm starving."

"We are too, Daddy." They sit in the dining room and Levy brings out plates of vegetarian stew, a loaf of homemade bread, and portabella mushrooms stuffed with goat cheese, parsley, basil, and ground pine nuts. They talk for hours over the savory food, and they finish two more bottles of wine before turning in.

Out of respect for Levy, Dan decides it best to stay in the guest bedroom, leaving Chiara to sleep alone in her room.

The next morning, Dan wakes to the wonderful aromas of fresh ground coffee and cinnamon. Peering out of the guest room window toward the majestic landscape outside, he feels for the first time in years that he is part of a family. He reflects on his parents. *Mom always baked me apple pies. I miss her—she would love Chiara.* He picks up his journal and scratches a few lines. The poem creates the shape of a vessel.

The smell of cinnamon
Makes me feel free
Warmed like a child in early spring
Running into the kitchen
Sweaty, muddy, bloodied knees
Healed with the fragrance of apple pie
Encrusted by her love

After finishing the verse, he showers and goes downstairs. Chiara and Levy are already having coffee. When Dan enters, Chiara slides out of her chair and greets him with a big kiss. Levy walks over to the oven, takes out a tray of cinnamon buns, and sets them on the table. Chiara pours Dan a cup of coffee, and the three of them devour the sticky, warm, buttery treats. Dan appreciates Levy's talents—a remarkable artist, cook, and father.

After a few more cups of coffee, Chiara announces, "I'm going upstairs for a shower."

"Take your time, honey. I'm going to show Dan the studio."

"OK. Sounds good. I'll come out when I'm finished," she says.

Dan and Levy set their coffee mugs in the kitchen sink and walk out the back door to a perfect sunny day. They stroll down a stone pathway toward an A-frame structure situated about a hundred yards from the house. It is surrounded by clusters of wildflowers and is light pine, with large North facing windows. The California light seems to nourish everything in her path.

The smell of oil paints and creativity permeates the studio. There are several easels set up with paintings at various stages of completion. Finished works are stacked along the perimeter. Some Levy explained he couldn't part with, while others he didn't think were good enough to be made public.

"Feel free to look around, Dan."

"Thanks. It's so great here."

Dan makes his way to some of the finished paintings and cautiously looks through them. He comes across a figure skating series featuring Chiara. They are action-packed images with lots of color. Levy captured her spins and jumps so well with his impressionistic style; it makes Dan feel like he is actually watching her skate. Dan then looks through another stack of canvases, where he finds a more somber, almost portrait-like work of Chiara sitting alone at the side of a rink with her head down. The painting undoubtedly captured her loss at nationals. As Dan examines it, Levy walks up next to him and utters, "Boy that was one sad day in our lives."

"Yeah, Chiara told me about some of this, but we never get too far before she just doesn't want to discuss it any further."

"Well, I guess it's good that she talks about it at all. I bet she never told you what took her off her game that day."

"As a matter of fact, she hasn't."

Levy cups his hand near his mouth and whispers as if someone was listening. "If you keep it between us, I'll explain. Maybe you could help her talk through it someday."

"Of course. I promise."

"Well, it was such a big day. She knew that if she just placed in the top three, she would have a spot on the Olympic team. The pressure was on, but she was ready...more ready than I've ever seen her. She had a great warm-up and was fifth in line to skate. While the judges were scoring the fourth skater, she got on the ice to loosen her legs." Levy shakes his own legs to emphasize his point. "So, she goes for a lap around the ice, and she just so happens to glance up toward the second level seats. Would you believe she saw her mother? Keep in mind there were thousands of people attending the competition. What were the chances? Neither of us knew her mother was going to attend. The whole thing was such a shock. You could literally see Chiara's persona melt into the ice, and while she tried to regain her composure, by the time her music started, her nerves were not set, and she lost focus and made mistakes. I'm sure her mother just wanted to see her skate, but that woman has injured Chiara in so many ways. I can't even talk about it. I'm not sure seeing her mother or losing the competition caused more trauma."

"It sounds so horrible. Why did you decide to even paint this scene?"

"It was the only way that I was able to cope with the loss myself. I needed to purge the whole thing from my own psyche. So, I painted this damn canvas with every ounce of emotional energy my body could muster." Levy emphatically shakes the painting before catching himself, where when he does, he gingerly sets it back on the floor. "I hope that someday Chiara can look at that painting and think of the whole thing as a transition in her life. All things change, Dan. All things change. Perhaps dealing with loss is the greatest teacher of gain. Kind of the yin-yang of the universe, right?"

They both agreeably nod at Levy's aphorism before repositioning the other paintings back to their original spots. As they move to the front of the studio, Dan browses at some of the other mostly unfinished works. "It looks like you have made some transitions yourself, Levy. These paintings are a very different style. Very abstract. The colors are beautiful; what were you trying to capture with these?"

"Oh, those aren't mine. They are Chiara's. When she was a kid, she would paint with me sometimes. Strangely, she is much better than I am. When she did those, she told me she was trying to paint energy and connect it to an underlying spiritual significance. Huh, she was only like twelve at the time."

"Wow. She is blessed with so many talents."

"Yes, she is. I'm so proud of her."

Chiara enters the studio and interrupts their discussion. "Hey, you two. What do you think of Daddy's paintings?"

"They're phenomenal, and so are yours."

With an embarrassed smile. "Oh, those old things... please." She does a three sixty around the room. "Daddy, show me some of your new works. It feels like forever since I've been back here."

"Take a look at this one." Levy guides Chiara to an easel where he has a sketch developing. Dan sees they could use some private time and asks if they mind if he uses the telephone. "Of course, son. There's a line in the kitchen and one upstairs."

"Great. Thanks."

Chiara says, "Then maybe we can go exploring when

you're finished with your call. Do you want to go over to the beach and caves? It's beautiful over there."

"Good idea," says Dan. He walks out of the studio.

"All right, so what were you guys talking about, Daddy?"

In an aloof tone, "Oh nothing..." Chiara knows that's code for them talking about her.

"I thought so. What do you think of Dan?"

"I think he's wonderful. I can see how much he cares for you. I also like the person you are when you two are together. I am very happy for you, princesse. You deserve a good guy."

Chiara hugs her father and says, "I've always had the best man, Daddy."

Levy gently kisses her forehead with pride. "You are my masterpiece, young lady."

Fifteen minutes later, Dan comes back into the studio wearing his black Chuck Taylors. "You ready to go?

"Sure am."

"Would you like to come with us, Levy?"

"No...you kids go ahead. I'm going to do some things around here. Maybe work on that sketch a little more."

"See you in a few hours." Chiara gives Levy a kiss.

~~~

Delano

When Del arrives at the nursing home, his father is using the toilet. Two aids stand at his side and coach the shit out of him before wiping his ass with a big ream of toilet paper. Del waits on a soft, high-backed chair while his father gets a new diaper. From there he and the aids help
~~~

him back into the wheelchair. Del guides the chair outside so his father can take in some fresh air. Looking down over the chair, Del notices how large his dad's head appears, unbalanced like an oblong stone on his skinny toothpick of a neck. His shoulders and cheeks are sunken, wasting right before everyone's eyes in a cachectic demise. Del positions his father so he faces the trees and the cloud formations clustered over the hills surrounding the facility.

Del knows that it can't be long. With sadness, he looks at his father's profile and hopes it just happens in his sleep—a calm, peaceful transition that protects him from pain. His father broke his nose after his most recent fall. It left him with bent eyeglasses and a bright, purple orb around his eye. His dad tries to assume a comfortable posture in the wheelchair, but despite his best efforts, he can't seem to find a suitable position. The constant pressure of sitting on his bony pubis is irritating.

Del asks his father if he sees the butterflies. "Yes. Ha, there they are," he says. The problem is the butterflies are on the far right, his dad is looking left.

"Sure is a nice day out today, isn't it?"

"Oh yes, it's beautiful," his father says. His words are uttered softly, and Del is relieved to hear an appropriate answer.

"How about a snack, Dad?" Del hands his father a banana and a huge cup of water, trying to stave off dehydration and hypokalemia, recently indicated on one of the lab reports. Del learned about electrolytes in his physiology class last year. Even though he only got a B minus for a grade, he still felt like he learned a lot, despite the professor being such an arrogant dick.

Del watches his father eat the banana. With small

bites, initiated by his two top middle teeth, he mechanically shortens the white stalk, like a beaver on a log. His dad always loved food, and watching him enjoy the banana has Del thinking back to Sunday roast beef dinners when he was a kid. He remembers his father always eating one or two slices of beef before pouring gravy over a few slices of bread, while everyone else was enjoying a second or third helping of beef. Del thought the gravy-over-bread dish was cool at the time. It was only just recently that he realized his father was trying to be sure there were enough cuts of meat for everyone else at the table. At the time, Del did not appreciate the sacrifices his father had made. Now as a young man, watching this old man—no, HIS old man...die...he knows, for the first time, what it takes to be a GOOD man. It isn't about some patriarchal power play—like so many of his feminist professors were writing about. It is instead about providing. It's about doing quiet and subtle acts of kindness that a family could always count on. Without a formal education or college degree, his father had been his greatest teacher.

His dad starts to look for something to wipe the stickiness of the banana from his hands. Del hands him a wet towel, and he cleans them in his OCD manner.

"I have to dof frei chze."

"What?"

I have the hathded." He rubs his hand along the bottom of his belly. Del knows that's his signal to use the bathroom again. "You just went."

"But, I have to..."

Del wheels him back inside to use the toilet. The aids come in to help him pee. Now, Del does his own wiping—his tears with his shirtsleeve.

~~~

Dan

Chiara and Dan arrive at Avila Beach. The air smells like cotton candy, and the sun is yellow and full. Dan is struck by the gorgeous rocky landscape interrupted by a few houses and shops lining the shore. The shady paths toward the water have sparse vegetation sprouting in all directions. Rays of light accentuate the red, brown, and green hues of the large mossy rocks—jutting their jagged heads out of the aqua blue of the Pacific. Separated by pockets of water, the scattered boulders are slapped by small waves. As if to say this place should only be liquid, the water punishes the rocks with erosion, renewing the sand with primordial fecundity.

Kayaks bob up and down with the waves while a cool breeze comes off the water with an invigorating freshness. Children are building sandcastles with small buckets in front of the long pier. Holding hands, Chiara and Dan take in the marvelous views.

"This is just how I remember it," says Chiara. "Daddy and I would come here when I was in middle school. I have such fond memories of it all."

"I can see why. It's beautiful." Dan pauses, "I think it's the light, it's like California has a totally different sun than Boston. I'm really noticing it on this trip."

"You're right, it does. It's kind of weird. I never thought about it growing up."

"It's like everything in life. You don't pay attention to things when you're around them all the time. Hey, are you ready to give me a tour of the sea caves?"

"Yes, from what I remember, we can get to a couple
~~~

from this trail." After a short hike, "Hey, there's one, let's go in."

"Wow, it's a little strange here," he says. "Do you hear that?"

"Hear what?"

"The echo. Listen, Chiara, Chiaraa, Chiaraaaaaa...Your name will bounce off these walls forever. The nymph that you are."

"Nymph, huh? OK, big guy, or should I say, Narcissus?"

"That's truer than I would like to admit. It's like we're in a womb."

"God, you come up with the strangest thoughts. Hey, let's go kayaking. I think there's a rental shop down the beach a little."

"All right. I guess if you've seen one cave you've seen them all." They stroll over to the shop. After picking out the perfect boat and signing their lives away on the risk contract, they hoist the kayak over their shoulders and carry it to the water's edge. Chiara gets in her seat while Dan awkwardly pushes them afloat from the shore. After they get used to the unsteadiness of the vessel, they paddle a little further out.

He asks, "How come I'm doing all the work?

"That's because I'm navigating." She laughs.

God, I need a break," he says while trying to catch his breath. He rests the oar across his lap and shakes out the burn in his arms. "Chiara, I was thinking, when you graduate, I would really like it if we could work together. You know, I need to keep writing to earn a living—the future wife and everything."

With a wide-mouthed grin, "I think that would be

awesome, but I don't think we would ever get any work done."

"That's true, at least based on your paddling performance."

"You seem to be getting me where I need to go just fine." She leans back and kisses him.

He whispers in her ear, "Ms. Dawson, where would you like to reside? Do you want to stay on the east coast or come out west to be closer to your father?"

"I don't know. I just want to be wherever you are."

"Well, we'll figure it out as we go along, hopefully for the rest of our lives." Dan stretches further forward and continues to kiss her neck. He almost tips the boat over.

"Careful, big guy. Don't flip us. There's no one to save us."

"I'll save you. Like...Magnum PI."

"OK, but I'm sure glad you don't have that ugly mustache."

"Hey, let's paddle over toward those rocks," he says.

"Sounds good. I feel like I'm getting sunburnt out here anyway."

"Wait, is that a seal?"

"Yeah, there are a lot of them around here."

"It must be a nice life, being a seal. It's like they're on a permanent vacation—eating, swimming, and sunbathing." Dan barks.

"Is that your mating call?"

He barks again before leaning forward to lick her salty shoulder. She smells like coconut.

Shivering from his tongue, she says, "Maybe I'll sneak into your room tonight."

"Make sure you knock. I wouldn't want to be indecent."

"Stop talking and get paddling. I'm burning up here."

"OK, but that thing in your hands...it's called an oar...it would help if you used it."

"What's that? I didn't hear you," she giggles.

Dan lovingly shakes his head and slowly paddles them back to shore.

***

When they arrive home, Levy senses their ethereal buzz. "So, you two, how was it?"

"Magical," says Dan. "It's just so beautiful here."

"God, I'm thirsty," utters Chiara as she walks into the kitchen.

"Want a drink, Dan?"

"Yes, please." They guzzle two huge glasses of ice water.

"Daddy, remember when we used to go kayaking?"

"How could I forget, honey? They are some of my best memories."

"Me too. Man, I'm starving," she says. "How about we do the cooking tonight, Daddy?"

Levy appreciates her caring offer. "I would very much enjoy that. We have all kinds of stuff in the fridge."

"Great, give us a few, and we will get the show on the road. Would you like anything special?"

"Anything is fine. You know I like just about everything. Other than lima beans..."

"I remember that." She giggles.

After two hot showers, Chiara and Dan start to prepare a vegetable frittata with fresh roasted peppers and potatoes. While the kids cook, Levy daydreams near the large picture window. He's thinking about Chiara's mom, wondering what it would be like if she were there too. This prompts him to relive his resentment towards her; how he more often than not would set the dinner table for two instead of three, trying to explain mommy away by telling Chiara that she was helping people see the world. He starts to choke on his own bitterness.

Chiara asks from the kitchen, "Hey, Daddy. Want some wine?"

"Oh, yes...yes that sounds great, honey." She carries a tall glass over to him. "Thanks. It sure smells good in there."

"I hope it tastes good. We'll be ready in a few." She goes back into the kitchen, where she's talking a mile a minute with Dan—a signature chattiness stemming from her childhood. Levy listens in. He has always loved her animated stories, her excited maturity, her mannerisms. It brings him back to their long Sunday pasta dinners together, when he never got a word in with her either.

"Food's ready," she calls out.

"OK." Levy walks to the table. "Wow, yum...this looks great guys," he says while taking his seat at the head. A toast, "To the both of you for bringing life into these four walls."

"Salute."

"It looks like you guys had a fun time exploring today. Mmm, this is delicious by the way."

"We sure did. It was Dan's first time in a kayak."

"Glad to see you survived. Chiara gets a little wild with the oar."

"That's for sure, even though she doesn't use it much." Dan laughs at his own joke.

"Yeah...fella, not that funny. And who almost tipped us, huh?" Chiara playfully pokes at Dan's arm. She looks over at Levy. "Did you paint today?"

"I sure did. I put some color down on that new sketch. I must say, it's comin' along."

"Can't wait to see it. Dan, tell Daddy the good news about your book."

"Yeah, before when I used the phone, I called my publisher. They told me that my book just sold out of Barnes and Noble. They are going to print another fifty thousand copies. I'm also being invited to discuss it on a couple of morning TV shows. We actually have to go to San Diego tomorrow. I was invited to do an interview. I'm really excited."

"Well, that is great news. You deserve this success. A toast to realizing your dreams for the two most special people." Their glasses cling like hand bells.

Chiara kisses Levy on the cheek. "I love you, Daddy."

He says in return, "How did I ever get so lucky, princesse?" They eat every crumb of dinner and move to the living room to listen to some of Levy's favorite record albums. Within minutes, Chiara is asleep on the couch, tired from her day at the beach.

They don't want to wake her, so Levy and Dan move back to the kitchen. Over a few beers: "Levy, I need to ask you something."

"Shoot."

Sitting upright in his chair: "I would like your blessing to ask Chiara to marry me."

"Holy cow. Are you serious? Wow..." Levy takes a deep breath. "This is great news. I think you two are perfect together. Of course, you have my blessing." Levy hugs him.

"Pheewwwww, I was so nervous asking. Thank you...I promise to treat her with all the love and respect she deserves."

"I know you will...I know you will." They hug again. "When were you thinking about asking her?"

"I think...next month. I want to surprise her with something she will never forget."

Levy says, "I'm so happy. I can barely talk." They clank their bottles together. "I'm so thrilled to have been able to spend this week with both of you. I wish you didn't have to go to San Diego tomorrow."

"I wish we could stay longer too. Why don't you come and spend time with us in Boston?"

"I might just take you up on that, young man. Ah...Dan, one more thing. Was Chiara excited about going to San Diego? I worry that it might open up some emotions in her."

"Yes, she told me she wanted to show me where she learned to skate. She seemed happy about it all though."

"Good, keep your eye on her. She's everything to me, son."

~ 3 ~

Chiara

Chiara was emotional after they left her father. First noticeable in San Diego, her melancholy worsened when they made it back to Boston. Dan was well aware of her sad disposition and desperately wanted to help. The conversation he had with Levy regarding Chiara's mother was still very fresh in his mind, and he thought it would be helpful if he could talk through the situation with her. He approaches Chiara a few nights later. Over dinner, he says, "Tell me more about your mom."

"What? Please. I don't really want to talk about her."

Their chewing becomes amplified over an avoidant and uncomfortable silence. She nervously says, "Why do you want to talk about her anyway?"

"I don't know. I'm just curious about it all."

She fidgets in her chair. "This conversation just seems

so out of nowhere. It's kind of random, don't you think?"

Dan can see that she is starting to get upset. "We don't have to, if it's..."

"Well, like what? Memories...of her?"

"Anything at all."

She offers, "OK...well, she used to smell like citrus. Orange...actually."

With a curious inflection. "That sounds like a good memory."

"It is. I used to like to climb up on her lap and smell the crease of her neck. I remember falling asleep on her shoulder a lot too. I also used to like grabbing her ears. They were cold. They felt nice in my hand."

"They all sound like great memories."

"Yeah. You know, I kind of worshipped my mother when I was a little girl. We used to do a lot of things together...when she wasn't traveling and all. It seems like such a long time ago, it's almost not real." Chiara develops a strained expression on her face.

"That's got to be very hard. Have you ever talked with her...you know, since she left?"

"No, not really. The last time she tried to contact me was after my loss at nationals. She sent me a letter, something like, 'Chiara, it's your mother. My heart is heavy with grief over your loss. I am so sorry. I know it's been quite some time since we have talked, but I am here for you if you might want to...I could fly in.' I never answered...even though her words sounded so sincere. In a strange sort of way, I wanted her to suffer. I feel so resentful towards her, Dan. I feel like she's ruined me."

Dan kisses her forehead and pushes a few loose strands of hair away from her face. "It's all right to feel that way. I just wish things were different for you."

With an unguarded look in her teary eyes, "I know...thanks. Like I said, most of the time I don't think about it. I'm OK." Dan moves over and pulls her close to his chest with a secure hug. She rests her ear over his heart for a few minutes and listens to its rhythmic reverberations.

"How about some wine?" He goes into the kitchen and pours them two tall glasses of pinot from a bottle they brought back from Napa. He sets one in front of her on a coaster on the coffee table. Next to the glass sits a pile of architect-like sketches that Dan had used to illustrate his vessel philosophy. Chiara glances at the drawings and studies their artistic qualities with appreciation. They are drawn in pencil and reminiscent of Chagall. She leans forward and sips her wine. She is interested in the sketch showing two vessels holding hands, like a small version of *The Youth Circle*. "What does this one mean?"

"If I could only draw," he says. "It's my version of love—it's symbolic of us." He takes her finger and traces over the sketches. "See, do you feel it?"

"Yes, I do. I'm so thankful we are in the same circle," she says.

"Me too, but it's not a closed circle. See, it's an enso... never quite closed...infinite." They kiss. When they pull apart, Dan seems off in another world.

"You seem so distracted. What are you thinking about now?" she asks.

"I don't want to be a pain in your butt, but I have to say something. I know you don't want to hear it, but I think you should try to talk with your mom."

"Why is this such a thing for you tonight?"

"I've been thinking about it since we were in California. Her ghost is haunting you. You can't wait for her to fix what's broken. You must do it yourself. Just please think about it. The hurt of missing her has poked such a big hole in you; your energy is deflating like air from a flat tire. I want to help you stop the leak."

"Where's this coming from? Did Daddy put you up to this?"

"No, it's not like that. It's just that being back at your house and then...San Diego...well, it made me aware of your mothers' absence in your life. I know it's hard, but I think it could help you find some peace if you reached out to her."

"I don't know. I have to think about it. God, it's been like...twenty years."

"I realize it's been a long time. Just think about it, please. I'll do whatever I can to support you through it all." He lets the topic go and senses she is relieved to stop the discussion.

"What do you want to do?"

"You wanna watch *The Godfather*? I rented the video."

"Yeah, that sounds fun. I've only seen it fifteen times," she says.

"Ha, ha. Good, then you'll catch something new this time." He gets the movie started in the VCR. They watch a few scenes and dose off after Michael kills Sollozzo and McCluskey and moves to Sicily. They sleep soundly in each other's arms on the couch.

The next morning, Chiara wakes with her head stuck to Dan's sweaty shoulder. She quietly unglues herself from their tiny den and tries not to wake him while she gets ready for work in the bathroom. After she dresses and applies a light coat of blush, she thinks about their conversation. On her way out, she kneels and kisses his forehead after lovingly admiring his handsome face. She rubs her fingers along the shallow crow's feet around his eyes. He barely budges before saying, "Good morning, gorgeous lady."

"Hello, sleeping beauty. Sorry, if I woke you."

"Oh, you didn't. I was up. I just had my eyes closed."

"Yeah, sure you were." She hugs him.

"Hey, don't forget I have a lecture tonight. I won't be home until eight," he says.

His warm breath tickles her ear, a ploy he likes to use to arouse her. In a sexy, playful voice, "I remember, Professor. Maybe when you get back, I can try for some extra credit." She grabs his crotch and teases his hardness. Coyly, "Well, gotta go, can't be late for work."

"Oh...well...but...I'll try to leave early...OK...love ya," he says.

"Me too."

She walks directly from the apartment to Dunkin' and buys a take-out. She gets to the gallery a few minutes early and takes a few sips of coffee as she settles in. Despite having a slight headache, she immediately gets involved in the busy work of billing and mailings. After addressing a tall stack of pamphlets to some of the gallery regulars, she takes a break. She walks over to the painting of her and her mom and studies it closely. It sparks many memories, some fond, but all complicated by the pain of abandonment. She realizes she would need to pull every ounce of strength from her inner core to even try to reconnect with her mother—an emotional triple Axel of sorts. She is worried though, that it all may just be a waste of time. She also considers how reaching out to her mom may impact her father. Incapable of drawing any conclusion about what to do, she goes back to the escritoire and addresses more brochures.

After work, she doesn't want to be alone while Dan is at school, so she decides to kill some time at Daisy Buchanan's. She chooses the end stool closest to the door. It is without a back and slightly wobbly. She orders a pint of Dan's favorite, Pete's Wicked Ale, and takes a huge gulp. It's dark and smoky, just like the subterranean watering hole it's being served in, four steps below street level. Her graduate school friends would often party there late night, but at happy hour, it was generally a business crowd. She looks out the window as she drinks, mesmerized by shoes scurrying down Newbury. After striking up a few conversations with people around the bar, she goes through a few more pints. Daisy's is a good place to reflect, almost like a church, lit with stained glass bottles of bourbon and scotch. She knows Dan loves it there and wishes he didn't have to work so late this evening.

Soon, the Wicked Ale starts to open up her thinking. As it leaks into her neurons, she feels an added sense of warmth. The tall bottles on the liquor rack start to take on human form. They become skating fans. The feeling intensifies...white liquor, black liquor, all the spirits chant her name with equal power. Then a tall bottle stands out from the rest; the Frangelico—it glares at her and seems to whisper sage advice. She finishes her pint and makes her way back to Dan's after stopping for a greeting card. When she gets there, she scribbles a note in the card with one of Dan's pencils.

Dear Mom,

I am not sure where to start. The last time I saw you was right before my fall at nationals. As you might imagine, that was very traumatic for me. In fact, it was the second biggest loss of my life. I am sorry I never did respond to your letter. Now that I am a little older, I feel there are things we need to discuss. I would like to see you and think I need to have some relationship with you to be a happier person. If you could find some time, maybe we could meet up and talk, perhaps over brunch or something. I would be glad to travel to wherever is convenient for you.

Mom, I am unable to understand why you left us. I guess if I could just wrap my head around it, I could move on to a better place. I hope we can find time to meet.

Sincerely,
Chiara

P.S. Maybe we can even make cookies together, like we used to when I was a kid.

P.P.S. I thought you should know that I have fallen in love with someone. His name is Dan. I hope that I can tell you all about this (if)when I see you.

She reaches into her purse and pulls out the letter her mom sent her after nationals. She copies the address from the return label and tosses the card in the corner mailbox. She hopes she is still at the same Argentinian address.

~~~

Zach

Friday finally arrives and I meet Pergo at his office 'round nine. We talk about my generally borin' week before turnin' the conversation over to Megan. We review his plan for me to tell 'er about my condition. He thinks I should also show 'er some of the articles written about my exhibition and my arrests. I explain to him, "I'm less worried about that stuff than I am about my...it's embarrassin', you know. Oh, hey there, I'm Zach, and I'm a bit of a nut. What's she gonna think? I'd hit the trail if I heaard that from her."

"It's the right thing to do, Zach. If she's not accepting, then it would be best to have it all come out in this early stage of your relationship. Explaining your past to her is the only option."

"OK. But..."

He cuts me off, "Don't worry. Everything will be all right."

I leave his office to get ready. I stop at Deluca's and buy a can of citrus furniture polish, fresh green pears, OJ, and a bag of sweet and salty mixed nuts. When I get home, I wash one of the pears and bite into its wet flesh. Inside, sits a tiny, brown worm, which I quickly cut out with my favorite silver butter knife from that pissass Dorchester five and dime. I enjoy the sweet nectar, and after chewin' around the core, flip the stem and seeds into the garbage. I really want to make a good impression on her, so I clean. At about two, the phone rings.

"Hello." She sounds upset. "What's wrong?"

"I have bad news. I am not going to be able to come for
~~~

the weekend. My mom just fell down the stairs and injured her ankle. My dad needs my help with the B & B. I am so...so sorry. I'm so disappointed...I just don't..."

"Oh, it's aalright...don't worry...we'll arrange it for anothaa weekend. She OK?"

"I think so. Thanks for understanding. I will call you later so we can talk more. Everything is such a mess right now. We're gonna take her to the emergency room. Thanks again."

"OK. Yeah, you go ahead...best to your mom. Call me lataa."

I hang up the phone. My face feels flushed. The lights become bright...so bright. Who turned the lights on? The air smells like it's fryin'. I call Pergo. He'll be right over. "Hey, bring the doughnuts," I say.

Shhh...calm yourself little boy. No one will take you outaa the crib if you're cryin'. That itch, that fucking itch...it's baack...I'm drownin'...I'm alone. Do you hear it?...Glory, glory...hallelujah. Where's the choir? It tastes so bitter...no, I don't waant any. Don't make meeeee take it. Please, don't make me go. Shhhh...silence is golden. The itch moves...I hate kaleidoscopes.

A knock at the door.

"Goooood aaftaanoon. Geronimo...Hah, Geronimo rhymes with Pergo, GERONIMO...!"

"What are you saying?" he asks.

"She couldn't come. She has to help her dad. Like Liz helps Dick." Pergo's sweatin'.

"It's OK. I called Dr. Swanson. She's going to meet us at the hospital. I'm going to drive you, all right? Here's some water. Drink it slowly."

Next thing I know, I'm in a gown. I feel tired. My

elbows badly bruised. *Was I in a fight?* Wearily, "What happened?"

He's standin' next to Dr. Swanson with a worried look. "We're not sure. Have you been taking your medications regularly?"

"I think so...but I'm not sure. I feel so frickin' confused."

Dr. Swanson calmly asks," Zach, I want to conduct some tests. I have you scheduled for an MRI. Is that OK?"

Pergo follows with, "Don't worry, these kinds of tests are standard. We are concerned you might have bumped your head." A few minutes later, after a little valium, two staff types with big biceps and pink scrubs wheel me into a room with a giant camera. They look inside me. I hear 'em talkin'...they don't see anythin'.

They keep me overnight for observation, and I get discharged the next day. Pergo's nice enough to drive me home and helps me inside my place when we get there. My apartment smells good, like citrus. It's also nice and clean. Because the shades are turned down, I switch on the red-based ceramic lamp on the round table next to the couch.

"Let me find my phone. Can't remembaa wheaa I put it." I look around and finally find it in the kitchen, sittin' on the counter, dead without a battery charge. I plug it in and ask him, "Want a glaass of OJ?"

"I would love one."

I hand it to him, slippery with condensation along the outside. He pulls out a handkerchief from his pocket and wipes off the wetness. He then folds it into a square, using it as a coaster. He sits next to me on the couch.

"Don't let this situation with Megan trigger feelings of abandonment. As we talked about in our previous sessions, the trauma you experienced as a child can greatly be reflected in your behavior now. Psychological trauma is like water. It can erode your brainy rock, changing the direction in which your thoughts flow. You have to always be conscious of those thoughts and the triggers that can take you into the spontaneous rapids of confusion and panic."

I listen while I massage the front of my head. It feels stiff, 'specially 'round my temples. "I think I might be in love with her."

"Well, it's kind of been a short..."

"I just know...aalright...shoaart or not."

"OK, I certainly understand. I fell in love like that once. She occupies everything in my soul." He becomes silent, almost in a trance before startin' again. "Well, the stronger your feelings are toward Megan, the stronger your reactions will be when things like this happen. Nevertheless, you need to be patient. All of this is very new for you. You are just starting to reach out to people. I still think you have made great progress. You should call her. If you don't mind, I would like to spend the afternoon here with you and observe the interaction."

"I don't mind. Thanks for carin' enough to stay. Just gotta wait for my phone to chaarge."

Pergo finishes his drink and brings his glass to the kitchen sink where he rinses it out with water. We talk more about Maine. I show him some paintings which are dryin' in the second bedroom.

"These are fantastic...absolutely fantastic. You have such a great talent."

"Thanks, I enjoyed paintin' up there. It was just perfect. Especially with 'er."

"Well, why don't you see if your phone is charged and

give her a call."

I check it and the green light is on. I power it back up and find five messages. "Doc, I'm gonna call her. She left me some messages and she's worried."

"Go ahead. Just pretend I'm not here." After the second ring, she picks up. "Hi."

"Oh. I am so glad you called. I didn't hear from you and...well, I was worried that you were mad at me or something."

"How could I be maad at you? My phone just died, and I didn't realize it. Sorry. So how are things goin'?"

"Pretty good. My mom is doing a little better. She just has a bad sprain. But I have to tell you, I had a huge fight with her last night."

"I'm glad she's doing bettaa. What did you two fight about? Are you aalright?"

"We fought about me coming to visit you. She thinks it's too soon to visit a virtual stranger. I told her I'm an adult, and she needs to respect my decisions. I just do not want to hear that from her. I mean, I'm a fully grown woman. I just miss you."

"I miss you too. Cut 'er some slaack, she's probably jus' worried that I'm some sort of psycho or somethin'." I roll my eyes at Pergo.

"I know, you're right. It's just hard taking orders from my parents. What have you been doing?"

God, if she only knew.

"Just be thankful you have 'em. Me, I'm just puttin' some finishin' touches on some paintings. Nothin' special. Hey, I think you should go talk with your mom. I don't want to get between you two. Mothaas and daughtaas need to stick togethaa."

I get distracted by Pergo. He suddenly looks ill. His face is pale. He wipes his eye, like there's somethin' stuck in it.

In a reassuring voice, Megan says, "She'll get over it. Yeah, OK...I will talk to her...maybe later, after I don't feel so frustrated. I need to pray over it."

Always prayin'...

"Well...I know you will work it out." I look back over at Pergo. He still doesn't look good.

"I'm still hoping to visit you next week, no matter what she says. She should be more functional by then...at least physically...Ha, ha. So, how about I call you tomorrow after I get this sorted out better?"

"Sounds good." I kiss 'er through the static of the receiver. When I hang up, I glance at him.

With a tense expression on his face: "I think the call went well."

"Yeah, me too. Are you feeling aalright? You look so white. Want some more OJ?"

"No, thank you. I'm fine. I'm just feeling a little tired. I should be going. Promise to call me if you need to talk or anything."

"I'm good. You go ahead. I am just going to haang out and get myself togethaa. Thank you for everything, Doc."

"You're welcome."

We man-hug as he departs. I'm a little worried about him. He jus' seems weird.

~~~

Chiara

The next thing she realizes, Chiara is sitting in a middle, coach seat, squeezed in on both sides by two middle-aged
~~~

men. On the aisle, reclines a priest in baggy, black and white garb. He has a cool demeanor but was warmly accommodating when Chiara crawled across him to squeeze into her seat. At the window sits a stout, balding man with a round, red face. He is wearing a green golf shirt and blue, plaid pants. He smells like cigarettes. After buckling up, she pulls her mom's note from her purse.

Dear Chiara,

I cannot tell you how happy I was to receive your card. I would love to spend time with you. How about we meet midway in the Maya de Riviera and do a spa vacation together—just the two of us. I took the liberty of purchasing you a plane ticket. It is enclosed in this envelope. If for some reason you cannot make it, leave a message at the hotel (their pamphlet is also enclosed). I will be checking in there daily and will arrive one day before you. I cannot wait to see you, honey. It has been much too long!!

Love,
Mom

The letter makes her fidget in her seat. While she is both excited and scared about seeing her mother, she reflects on how thrilled she was to receive such a prompt reply back from her. Maybe her mother does care. Chiara also reflects on how pleased Dan was about the news.

After an hour delay on the tarmac, they take-off. She tries to take a nap but is unsuccessful in the wake of the choppy air. To pass the time, she instead reaches into her purse and pulls out the Cosmo that she purchased at the airport magazine shop. She intently starts reading an article on female orgasms and wonders what they feel like. She imagines them like turbulence—falling...no control, a satisfying hard, jarring bump that makes you cheer when it all comes to rest. Her thoughts go to Dan. Though he is a caring lover, something seems missing from their sex life.

When she finishes the article, she dog-ears the page and carefully sets the magazine back into her purse before gazing out of the window towards the puffy expanse of the pinkish sky. She shares some casual conversation with her row companions and washes down a small bag of pretzels with a spicy Bloody Mary. Time elapses quickly, and she is soon buckling up for landing. The plane makes a steep descent on the short Cancun Airport strip before abruptly stopping near the terminal. Seconds after coming to a halt, the scurrying percussion of overhead compartments is heard throughout the cabin. Among the snare-like rhythms, Chiara stands on her toes and struggles to reach for her bag. Father Kelley, who is unsuspectedly tall, helps guide it down.

"Thank you, Father."

"You are welcome, young lady."

They exit the plane and wait in customs together. After making small talk, they split ways at the main section of the terminal, where they are swarmed by a bustling mosquito nest of tour guides and vendors.

"Have a great trip, Father."

"You too. Have a blessed day." He makes a sign of the cross as they part. Along with the other overly hydrated tourists, Chiara stops off in the lady's room to freshen up before the shuttle ride to the resort.

She travels with a few different groups. In the last row, two parents with dark circles under their eyes sit squashed together with their preteens. A retired couple is spread out next to her in the middle row, and a few single guys on a golf outing are horsing around in the front, when the driver, a short man with coal black hair, finally gets in and offers them margaritas. Chiara accepts the tangy treat, takes a few sips, and puckers her lips from the salt and lime. She becomes entranced with the intense Mexican sun, and the second cocktail in two hours leaves her with a slight buzz.

The ride has an intensity to it. As the van passes through the outskirts of Cancun, the rural poverty of the country becomes obvious. This, along with the driver repeatedly staring at her in the rearview, makes her fidget. She can't help noticing the absent gaze in his yellow eyes, like over-easy, fried egg yolks dripping into neighboring whites. He stops when he realizes Chiara is aware of his gawking, pretending to redirect his attention towards the road.

About an hour later, they arrive at the resort, where she cautiously exits through the side door, lowering her skirt to cover up her legs as she slides out of her seat. The driver acquires her bag from the back of the van, and she provides him with a modest tip, carefully not allowing skin-to-skin contact while placing the greenbacks in his palm. He politely gestures as he utters thanks in an Eastern European accent.

The front of the resort is clay-colored with lush flowers in giant turquoise pots set along its portico. The cool, serene lobby has off-white tile floors, which reflect streaks of glimmering light from the ceiling windows. In the center, people are gathered around an enormous fountain, circumscribed by green tropical plants and colorful flowers. Most of the lobby is enclosed by large glass patio doors, which open outwards to a grand terrace. Gigantic ceiling fans circulate the fresh beach air throughout the space. The tin and terra cotta sconces, combined with bright watercolors of tropical birds and fish along the walls, amplify the Latin vibe.

The clerk at the check-in desk seems to be expecting Chiara and efficiently directs her to the room. As far as she knows, her mom arrived yesterday. She carries her own bag to 1445 on the east side of the resort and stands outside the door taking a few deep breaths before knocking. “Mom, its Chiara,” she says after two strikes at the door. There’s no answer.

She tries knocking two more times before inserting the key. In an uncertain voice, she again calls out, but still no response. Hesitantly, she makes her way into the suite and places her bag on a black rod-iron table with a glass top. The room has an art deco flair and is painted in lime green. She looks around for her mom and notices the patio door is open. A salty breeze tickles the sheer, ivory drapery, allowing cast blue shadows to flicker on the sand-colored floor. The sun seems to hold a warm, molten presence outside, with its heat juxtaposed to the surreal coolness within the room. When she steps outside onto the patio, she sees her mother leaning over a garden of passion fruit, admiring fragrant vines lined with black and orange butterflies that look like tiny, winged zebras. She is like a child at play, holding large flower blossoms to her nose. Her long, blonde hair is dangling over her right shoulder, and she is wearing a sheer yellow and white dress, loosely concealing her slim, tan body.

Chiara walks toward her. In an inquisitive tone, she calls out, “Mom.” Chiara’s mother turns and drops the flowers to the ground when she realizes it’s Chiara’s voice. The air draws still as they take each other in. Like two elastic bands, almost stretched to a breaking point before again recoiling back toward one another, they meet in the middle with a vigorous, sweaty embrace. Sticking to one another and holding back the fearful quivers of solidarity, they hug tightly, until their breathing synchronizes. Chiara’s mother pauses, and she holds Chiara back at arm’s length, while taking her in from head to toe. Both have swollen eyes from releasing deep springs within, unfiltered salts and minerals from the core of things. The silence breaks, “Chiara, you have grown into such a beautiful woman.”

Wiping a tear from her eye, Chiara muffles, “Thanks... umm...you look really good too...Mo...”

Excitedly: “I’m so glad you came.”

“‘Em, well it was kinda my idea.”

“I know, I know...but still...thanks, honey. You have no idea how much this means to me. Come on, you want to go up to the patio?”

They walk slowly in stride toward the suite, where they sit on wicker chairs with pillows decorated in vertical striped patterns of blue and gold. The sultry afternoon heat prompts a dehydrated effect on their lips.

“Do you want a drink, honey? I have virgin daiquiris chilling in the refrigerator.”

“That sounds great, Mom. This heat really does make you thirsty.”

Chiara’s mother returns with two thick-rimmed

glasses and a large icy pitcher. She pours them both a glass of the strawberry coolness.

"I'm so glad to see you, I don't even know where to start. Your letter really hit me hard. I...I didn't think you would ever want to see me again."

"I didn't think I ever wanted to see you again, either. But...well, over the past few months, I've been thinking... there are so many things I don't understand. I'm hoping this trip can resolve some of my issues...give me some peace." Chiara washes her words down with a huge gulp.

"Honey, you know, sometimes situations aren't exactly how they appear."

Chiara skeptically dismisses her words while downing the remainder of her glass. In an abrupt, avoidant tone, "Yeah, and sometimes they are. Do you mind if I take a shower? I feel dirty from the trip."

Avoiding confrontation: "Of course, honey." Her mother directs her to the bathroom and returns to the patio. She pours herself another drink and blows off a big sigh as she resettles back into her chair. She feels the immensity of the journey ahead. How will these gaping wounds ever begin to scab over?

After a few minutes, Chiara comes back to the patio wrapped in a white, terry cloth robe with a small, green towel around her hair.

"Feel better?"

"Yes, thanks. I am sorry for being short with you. I know this is hard for you too."

"It's fine. Yes, I think this is going to take a while. I'm so happy to see you, no matter what."

Chiara doesn't respond. They both sit quietly for a few minutes watching the large palm tree leaves flutter with the breeze.

"How's Argentina?" She unwraps the towel from her hair. "Where do you live there?"

"It's good. I don't live too far from the Plaza de Mayo in Buenos Aries. It's a small apartment, but comfortable."

"That sounds nice."

"Yes, it is. Buenos Aries is my home now. I've lived there for years...after, you know..."

"Huh, no...I don't know much about..."

"Yes, well...I hope to explain all of this to you. I have friends there. Mothers who lost their children in the Dirty War. We rely on one another...God, it touches me... because I know...I know...how those mothers feel—being without you and everything."

In a loud voice: "But you were the one who decided to leave, Mom."

"I know, honey, it's all so complicated. Look, we have the whole week to talk about this. Let's start slowly, a little at a time." She puts her face in her hands. Chiara sees her strain and remains quiet. "What do you say about grabbing a bite? You must be hungry after your flight."

In a hoarse voice: "Yes, I am a little."

"I was thinking the outdoor terrace restaurant. It looks so nice."

"Sounds great to me."

They go inside and dress. Chiara puts on a light blue skirt and a white tank. Her mother slides into a long, pink sundress, with knee-high slits along the sides. After they both apply a few dashes of Narcisse Noir (1911) from her mom's bag, they stroll along the boardwalk to the restaurant. The sun has almost completely set, and the ocean breeze leaves them with a slight chill, prompting Chiara's mom to drape the sweater she is carrying over

Chiara's shoulders. Flowering cacti with purple and red blossoms line the walkway, and people are having drinks at the beach bars all along the way.

A handsome, olive-skinned man seats them in the restaurant. He brings a short candle with a tall flame to their table on the second level balcony. It has an unimpeded view of the water. Like a van Gogh painting, the resort lights reflect off the small breakers in an illusory tone. Flamenco music plays across the crowded terrace. Chiara's mom orders another virgin daiquiri while Chiara sips on a glass of pinot grigio. They choose several small tapas plates for sharing.

"I would love to hear about this man in your life."

"Well, it's difficult to know where to start. He's a big part of why I wrote the letter to you. He thought we should try to connect." Chiara smiles at her mother. "Anyway, he's a really cool guy—very caring and smart. He's into literature and writing and is an ex-jock. He reminds me of dad a bit. Let me show you a photo." She reaches into her purse and pulls out some Polaroids.

"Wow. Very handsome. He sounds nice. What does he do for a living?"

"He's a professor of philosophy and psychology, which by the way, I am getting a graduate degree in. He just published a book on human relationships, *The Human Vessel – A Model for Interpersonal Interactions*. It recently made it on to the best sellers list."

"Oh my God, what a coincidence. Can you believe that my therapist just had me read that book? I loved it, and it really helped me deal with so many of my issues. He has such a good perspective using those vessels to represent personal interactions. Masters? Wow! Wait, are you dating your teacher?"

"No, no. It's not like that. He's at a different institution."

"I'm so happy you found such an interesting man. I am so impressed with how educated you have become. You always were incredibly intelligent...and now in lo..."

"Thanks...I'll never forget the day I met him. He came into the art gallery where I work and literally swept me off my feet. Since then, I feel like my life has forever changed. It's like he completes me."

"I am so happy for you, honey. It's so hard to find a true love."

"I know. It all happened so serendipitously. When he first came into the gallery, I saw him gravitate towards the painting Daddy did of us when I was a baby. It's being shown there. It was like a sign to me."

"Your father's paintings always did engage people. How's he doing anyway?"

"Dad's fine. I brought Dan home to meet him a few weeks ago, and they got along pretty well. Then we went to San Diego for a few days. It was so nice being back there. We drove through the old neighborhood and everything."

"Really? I have not been there for so long. How does it look?"

"Exactly the same. The entire neighborhood hasn't changed at all. Even the skating rink."

Chiara's mother sips her drink. "Did you see any of your coaches?"

"No, I didn't go in. I just showed Dan where I spent so much of my time."

"How about the Zoo or Balboa Park? Those were always your favorites when you were little."

"Yes, we had to spend a day there. We had such a great time."

"Mmm, try this dish, honey. It's delicious." Chiara sticks her fork into the ceviche, a medley of prawns and scallops in a citrus-spiced marinade accented with bold flavors of onion, lime, and cilantro.

"Yum, this is great. We don't get good Mexican food like this in Beantown."

"It sure is. I was thinking, how would you like to hike around the Mayan ruins a little this week?"

"Oh, that would be a lot of fun."

"Great, we can plan it all out tomorrow. I collected some tour pamphlets to look through."

The music grows loud, and they people watch as they finish their meal. After their plates are cleared from the table, the handsome host brings them two pieces of chocolate cake, made with special Mexican cocoa.

"Please, my gift for two gorgeous sisters," he says.

They giggle like crushing schoolgirls at his gracious compliment.

After dinner they return to their room. Chiara feels so cheerful, she calls Dan to tell him how great the day went. He doesn't pick up, so she leaves a message on his answering machine. After she hangs up, she walks into the kitchenette. "Goodnight, Mom. I need to get some sleep. I'm exhausted. See you tomorrow."

"Of course, honey." A few minutes later, Chiara's mother tiptoes into the bedroom and kisses her forehead. She tightly tucks the covers around Chiara's shoulders and whispers, "Good night. I love you." For Chiara, half-awake, it's a wonderful reminder of her childhood.

~~~
~~~

Dan

Leaning over his table, Chelsea says, "I'm so glad you were able to come tonight, Doc."

"You know I always love listening to you, Chelsea. As always, you jammed. Your originals are really deep."

"I felt a little flat. Did I sound that way?

"Not even close. You were right on. You looked good on stage, too. I like your skirt."

Chelsea adjusts the fabric around her hips. "Oh, thanks. I just wore this because it's so hot outside."

"I know. For this time of the year, it's so..."

"So, how come you're on your own? Where's Chiara? I thought you two were coming together."

"Oh, she's spending the week with her mother in Mexico."

"That sounds fun."

"Yeah, it's much needed together time. Hey, I thought Noah was coming...where is he?" Dan looks around the room.

"He called me right before the show and said he wasn't feeling well."

"That's too bad. I haven't seen him around school much. I was hoping to get to talk with him a little."

"You know Noah. He thinks he's dying with the slightest sniffle. I appreciate that you came though." She adjusts her skirt again.

"No need for thanks. I love listening to you." Dan sips his beer. "So, how have things been going on your end?"

She sits next to him. "Life is all right. I'm going through some things right now, though...you know, personal stuff." She has a serious expression.

"Do you want to talk about it?"

"I don't know. Maybe." Dan picks up his beer, and Chelsea circles her index finger in the small puddle of condensation that it leaves on the table. "I was dating this guy and...he just told me he is taking another job, in Phoenix, of all places. He planned it for a while and never bothered to mention it. It has me pretty bummed. I mean...he's leaving next week and just told me yesterday." She smears the little puddle of water around the table with her palm.

"Wow, that is sudden. Sounds like he didn't know how to break it to you. Maybe he was trying to spare your feelings or something."

"Well, this makes it even worse. I mean, he didn't give me any time to wrap my head around it. He also could have asked if I was interested in joining him."

"Would you have?"

"I don't know...maybe. I guess I could have transferred to Arizona State or something. I mean, we have been together for six months, which is long for me. I dig him. He writes songs."

"Well, maybe you can maintain a long-distance relationship. Sounds like you have a lot in common."

"That's what he said, but I just broke it off. You know long distance relationships never work out." She fixes her hair behind her ear.

"Just give it time. Anyway, men are like buses—another will be along in ten minutes."

"Ha, ha. Hey...want to go have a drink, Doc? I could use one to loosen up."

"Sounds good. How bout we hit Daisy's?"

"Perfect."

They exit the small venue on Huntington and walk the

few blocks to the bar. They are damp with sweat when they arrive. After they squeeze through a tight crowd of college kids at the door, they order a couple of drinks. It's even steamier in the bar.

"Hey, let's do this tequila shooter," says Chelsea. Sam the bartender hands them over the bar between two girls with big hair.

"Excuse me, ladies. Thanks, Sammy. Cheers," says Dan. Sam raises his own glass, signaling for the three of them to slug back the shooters. They chase them with cold Coronas. A few minutes later, they follow up with two more rounds, and then a repeat shortly after that. Dan turns to Chelsea in a buzzed voice, "I guess tequila and Corona are the right choi...ces since Chiara is in Mexi...Mexico, huh?"

"Definitely," says Chelsea while bopping up and down to the music. Slurring, "Hey, I love this s...s...song, let's dance." She grabs him by the hand and pulls him near the wall.

"You know, I don't da..." Before the words leave his mouth, Chelsea is up against his chest. He takes a step back and grabs her hand, encouraging her to spin. She does, but almost falls before he steadies her.

She leans into his ear, "Thanks, Doc. It's so slip...pery." The room grows louder as the DJ spins Prince. The shoulder-to-shoulder crowd dances vigorously. Chelsea's getting pushed back into Dan. Inadvertently, they find themselves in a slight grind with his hips against hers. With a warm breath, "God, this is fun. You're such a great dancer, Doc." They fall in sync.

"Hardly, the only thing I'm good at is sho...shots," says Dan in a drunken voice.

Leaning up to his ear, "I think you are great at everything...Dan. You don't mind if I call you, Da..." She leans in and kisses his cheek. "Maybe you haven't been told that enough." He likes the feel of her body, her musky smell. They lock eyes and kiss. He places his hand on her ass, squeezes, and pulls her firmly towards him. She is wearing a loose-fitting top, and he caresses her belly and the small of her back. They are one against the wall. She undoes his fly and rests her hand on him. He is hard. He wants her. She knows this. She is wet. She wants him. He knows this.

"No...NO...God, what are we...doing? We have to stop...this is so..."

In a slur, she says, "I'm sorry, D...This just got so...out of..."

"It's OK. It's OK. Look, I need to g...I just need to go. I think I'm goin' to be sick." He zips back up and darts through the crowd into the night air. He hurries to the alley behind the bar and vomits, causing a few rats to scurry away from their late-night dumpster snack. Despite the mugginess, he feels chilled. Leaning forward with his hands on his knees, he wipes his mouth and watery eyes after the fourth bitter chuck, empty in its release. He grips the wall and guides himself to his feet, oriented well enough to start zigzagging home down the Fairfield sidewalk. He finds his building twenty minutes later. After struggling up the stairs and unlocking his door, he falls to the floor and inventories his puke-stained shirt. The apartment is spinning, and he rolls to his side, desperately wanting it to stop. The merry-go-round holds him hostage for hours.

Somewhere along the way, he crawls into the bedroom

and climbs on the bed. He sees the red light blinking on the answering machine. He hits **PLAY MESSAGE** after struggling to the nightstand.

"Hi sweetheart, it's me. I had such a wonderful day with my mother. I can't thank you enough for encouraging me to reach out to her. I hope you are doing well. I'll call you tomorrow. I miss you and love you forever. You're my soulmate."

~~~

Chiara

The next morning, Chiara's mother wakes early. She plans to share her story with Chiara and knows it's going to be an emotionally demanding day. She quietly makes herself a cup of coffee in the kitchenette and proceeds outside to a small flower garden adjacent to their suite. She notices a few reddish-pink Hibiscus pedals being weighed down with droplets of dew. It prompts her to reflect on how her absence affected Chiara. With her coffee mug in hand, she strolls along the quiet beach. She enjoys the forgiving softness of the sand beneath her toes. The tide is low, and she has a sense of being the sole inhabitant on the planet.

An hour later, Chiara wakes and dresses in an extra-large, red BU sweatshirt and old gym shorts. She finds her mom on a beach chair outside, overlooking the water. The morning sky is yellow ashen. A refreshing easterly breeze leaves a chill in the air.

"Good morning."

"Good morning, honey. Did you sleep well?"

"Yeah, really peacefully. The sounds of the waves had me hypnotized."
~~~

"I hope I didn't wake you."

"No, not at all. I'm so used to getting up early to train for skating." Chiara flicks some sand from her leg.

"It's really beautiful here. I could look at the water all day."

"Me too. I love the freshness."

"Would you like a cup of coffee?"

"I sure would. I feel slow this morning," Chiara says.

"Ha, ha. Me too. Let's go up to the patio and have some. I always need at least two cups to get me going." Chiara waits on the patio while her mom goes inside for the coffee.

Hollering through the door. "Do you like anything in yours?"

"No thanks. I just like it black."

When Chiara's mother comes back outside, she is holding two tall mugs of coffee and several tour pamphlets. "So, take a look at some of these day trips, honey. They look fun...don't they?"

Chiara flips through the pages. "How about Tulum? They have great Mayan ruins there."

"Oh, that's a good choice. Then tomorrow, we could maybe go to Cozumel."

"That sounds perfect to me," says Chiara. They nod in unison.

Her mother says, "Well, then I'll make a reservation." She goes inside and telephones the concierge. She comes back to the patio. "We have an hour to relax before we get going. The van will pick us up right in the front of the hotel, at nine."

After some small talk, they go inside to pack for the day. They stuff bathing suits, hiking clothes, a few snacks, and drinks into a big shoulder bag. Chiara also packs her Polaroid camera. She wants to bring some photos back for Dan.

They board the tour van and sit close during the drive. They discuss their expectations for the day and are not disappointed when they arrive. They are amazed at the history and beauty of the architecture, especially how effortlessly it was incorporated into the natural landscape. After exploring for a few hours, they sit on two large boulders to rest their tired feet. They take off their shoes and pick small pebbles from their sneakers while sharing a bottle of water outside El Castillo.

At 2 PM, they reboard the van and get dropped off at Playa Paraiso. The heat is intense, and they cool themselves in the salty water after changing into their bathing suits. After a few strokes, they splash one another like children, laughing at the simplicity of it all. They stay in until their fingers shrivel, and when they make it back to the sand, they recline on warm rocks and absorb the sun.

"Chiara, I can't even begin to describe how wonderful this day has been for me. I know I can never get all those days that I missed from your childhood back, but for me, today has meant so much."

"Me too, Mom. Today reminded me of when you used to take me to the beach when I was a little girl. Remember the green sunhat that you used to make me wear? God, I hated that hat."

"I know, but I didn't want you to get sunburnt, honey."

"I realize that...but green?"

"Your dad picked it out. He thought it would be an easy way for us to spot you among the other children. He was right. You did stand out. The absurdity of it all." The sun weighs on their eyelids, prompting an urge to nap. As they start to melt into the landscape, Chiara's mom catches a second wind and decides it is a good time to try to explain things. She sits up in an erect posture and pulls a towel over her thighs.

"Honey, I have so much I want to share with you."

"Mom, you know what...let's just wait. We are having such a great day together. I don't want to ruin it with any intense discussions right now. Let's just talk about it over dinner."

"I think I need to explain, maybe more for my own sake. Do you mind if I get this off my chest?"

Chiara reluctantly agrees. "All right, I guess it would be good to just get it out. I mean that's what we're here for."

"Honey, it's hard for me to make sense of it all, and I'm not asking for forgiveness. I just want you to understand what happened. It's hard to tell you this...but when I left you...you and your father...it was because I fell...I fell in love with someone."

Chiara grimaces. In a disgusted tone, "Did dad know?"

"I don't know...I guess he did. It's all so surreal, like it never happened. When I was a flight attendant, you know...when you were a little girl...I was all over the world. I found myself on a similar flight schedule with this guy...this pilot, Robert. I was only in my twenties and never really dated anyone seriously, other than your father. Robert was a little older and worldlier, and he started to seduce me with his cavalier attitude towards life. He was so adventurous and handsome. God, he seemed to know exactly what he wanted and made it very clear that I was one of those things." Chiara's mom crosses her legs in a meditative pose under the towel. "I mean, I resisted at first, but then I started to fall for him. We were in all these exotic places together...he made me feel free. I felt trapped being a mom, and I think I was looking for something more. Your dad and I were kind of just going through the motions."

Chiara feels the blood rush to her face. In an angry, sarcastic tone, "Oh, that's great, Mom. Christ! How could you put some pilot in front of your own family? It sounds so sordid. No wonder you need a therapist." She makes a fist.

"Chiara, that's not the only reason why I have a therapist. It is much more complicated than that. Please, let me finish."

"OK. Sorry. It's just that listening to you say..."

"Robert was a military brat. He never seemed to have an anchor on family. I was with him for about a year, when I noticed him getting out of control...he...he became violent...he...started beating me." Chiara's mother crosses her arms.

"I hope you left him. He sounds like such an asshole. I guess you get what you ask for."

"No, I didn't leave him. Instead, I started self-medicating. See, he got me hooked on cocaine along the way...then we started using other stuff...I was a drug addict...just pitiful. You know, when I left you and your father, I always thought I would be back, that Robert was just a phase. But once I turned junkie, I completely lost my compass. Before I knew it, years had literally passed, and I was simply a pathetic human being. The ironic part is...Robert left me because he couldn't stand what I had become. The bastard never took any responsibility. He made it a point to never fly with me again." Chiara's mother starts to cry.

"What did you do? How'd you break the cycle?"

"Well, it took a long time. I constantly needed money to support my habits. I...I started to run drugs."

"Wait, what do you mean...you were a dealer?"

"I worked for a cartel."

"You can't possibly expect me to believe this when... wait, what cartel?" Chiara's eyes widen.

"It's true, honey. At the time, my main flight route was Southern California to Central America. It was hard given I was high all the time. But I kept working...spilled too many drinks on passengers...Ha, ha...if you only knew. Anyway, one day when I was at the airport traveling to the Tocumen Aeropuerto, this strange guy with a crew cut handed me a note that said he needed to talk to me over a matter of grave importance. At first, I thought it was a hoax and didn't pay much attention. Then he started to follow me away from the ticket counter. I turned to him and asked what he was doing. He told me to meet him in ten minutes at a bench near the coffee bar. I had a few hours to kill and was very curious, so I sat there to see if he would show up." Chiara's mother uses her hand to shield her eyes from the sun. "Sure enough, he did. He cautiously sauntered over to me, making it a point not to sit too close. He pretended to read the paper while introducing himself as Eric. He started by saying that everything he was about to tell me needed to remain quiet...or my life might be in jeopardy." She makes a shooting gun gesture with her hand. "He told me Robert referred me to him."

"Wait, Robert, also got you running drugs?" Chiara

kneels on her towel.

"Yes. Robert dragged me into it, but Eric was the driving force. He arranged everything. He was the connected one. They would load my suitcases up with the stash, and I would carry it in the overhead bins reserved for flight attendants before dropping it off in another city. They would give me an envelope with cash. I would use it to just buy more drugs."

"I...I don't know what to..." Chiara rubs her temples.

"Yeah, Eric had been running drugs through Central America for years. He was a pilot too...he met Robert in the Air Force. Then one day, everything changed...people started getting killed. He told me we immediately needed to go off the grid because our lives were in danger. Governments were even involved. I had no choice, so I hid out with him outside Panama City for about six months. One thing led to another...we developed a relationship and...well, that's where I conceived your half-brother." She gazes down at the sand.

"Wait. You lost me. What half-brother? I don't even know what you're saying," says Chiara.

"Yes honey, you have a half-brother. He was the cutest little thing. He had the most unique birthmark on his neck—a perfectly shaped Z." She points to her neck and traces the shape.

"What happened to him, Mom? Why do you say 'was'?"

"Well, I was so high all the time...I...I couldn't take care of him...Eric just took off one day. I mean, I...was forced to give him up to a Jesuit orphanage. It was terrible. I've never seen him after that. I pray every day that he found a good home...such an innocent little guy." She says in a desperate voice, "The nuns then got me into a rehab program. That's when I finally started to get well. I was already in my late-thirties and was a complete burnout. Without them, I'm sure I would be dead by now." She makes the sign of the cross after wiping her eyes.

Chiara is speechless. She has so many questions. Her mom looks to her for a reaction, but she realizes it's going to take some time for Chiara to digest all that she had heard. "That is where I am. I'm clean now and see a therapist. I have a lot of guilt, as you could imagine. I wanted to give something back, so I started working with those nuns; they do such important work with orphans and everything. That's why I stayed in Argentina. I'm trying to help other mothers, who like me, have lost their way. I'm so sorry, Chiara. I never should have...I never thought..." She reaches into her bag and pulls out a small plastic bag. Inside sits a clump of fine blonde hair. "It's yours. I clipped it before I left...when you were sleeping. I keep it with me wherever I go." They both break down.

"It's OK. Mom, it's OK..." Chiara leans in and tightly wraps her mother with her towel, almost an inverted image of Levy's painting.

***

It's soon time to catch the tour van back to the resort. After changing out of her wet bathing suit, the shivering Chiara puts her red sweatshirt back on. She and her mother make it back to the tour van five minutes before departure. Before they get in, Chiara's mother takes a Polaroid of her for Dan. Chiara poses with a big smile—the sunny glow of a happy young woman with a bright future and everything to live for.

~ 4 ~

Zach

When I arrive, he's on the bed with his left foot slightly danglin' over the edge. It's illustrative of his being, flaccid and barely with life. The sight of him makes my stomach sink, you know, like when a roller coaster freefalls down its first big drop. I'm not quite sure what is happenin' beyond what Dr. Swanson explained earlier. She thought it would be important for me to visit him and was nice enough to get me here...so here I am.

"Are you doing OK, Zach?"

"Yeah, it's just..."

"You can try to talk to him. We believe that people in a coma still have their sense of hearing preserved."

"Yeah, OK...I will...I don't..."

"Look, sit here for a few minutes. I know this is hard," she says.

I pull my chair pretty close to his bed. "Hey, Doc. It's

me." I reach out and pat his pale, dusty hand. It feels like ice. Even though I try not to, I weep at the sight of him. He looks so banged up.

"That's it. Keep going." Dr. Swanson encourages me by touching my back with calming circles.

"Hey umm, Doc. I...finally took your advice and umm...started reading a book last night. Hell, it was the first time since like...forevaa. I have to say it was sort of, you know...relaxin'."

Dr. Swanson says, "You're doing great. You know what...I'm going to let you two alone for a few—so you can visit in private. Do you think you would be comfortable with that?"

I look up at 'er from my chair after a big sniffle. "Yeah, that sounds good. I'm OK...I just wish..."

"I know, me too. But we are going to deal with this head-on, just like we discussed. I'm going up to my office to tend to a few odds and ends. How about I pick you up when I'm finished. Have the nurses page me if this gets to be too much."

"AAlright. I'll just hang heaa for a while. Thanks." She leaves the room, and I listen to the clicking of her heels echoing down the hallway toward the elevator. I push my chair sideways into a more comfortable position.

"Doc. Hey, ahh...so...it's me again...I don't know if you can hear me, but I want you to know that I wish ya..." I can't get the sentence out. I feel trapped and itchy in the metallic, sterile space and crumble into an almost fetal position and cry.

A couple minutes later, I get myself together after wipin' my eyes with my sleeve and everythin'. "You know, I think you're the closest...the closest thing to a fathaa...for me...I...mean." I get up and walk over to the window and look out for a few. I call out, "Oh yeah, the book—it's called *Anam Cara*. I don't know if you evaa read it, but it's the kind of thing you'd like. I mean the guy who wrote it is religious, but...well, Megaan recommended it to me...so it figaas."

Stupid fuck...what do ya think...he's gonna answaa? Well, maybe he can sense...

I go back to the bed. "Hey Doc, I can't wait for you to get bettaa. Don't forget we have to talk to Megaan togethaa, right? Hey, maybe you just need some rest right now. I'm gonna stay with you for a while. OK? Just sayin', 'cause I don't want ya to feel like you're alone or anythin'. Like you told me...we're all in this toget..." I sit again and lean back in the chair while tryin' to ignore the repeatin' pulsin' sounds of the monitors.

A few minutes later, there's a rufflin' at the door. I look over and watch this older guy come into the room. He takes off his baseball cap and gestures hello. He takes me by surprise, particularly with his modern style of dress—a flannel shirt and baggy, beige cargo pants. He goes directly to the head of the bed, which is slightly inclined. "How are you today, son?" He kisses Pergo's forehead before wiping a tear from his puffy eyes. He introduces himself in a raspy voice, "Hi there, I'm Levy."

"Hey...I'm Zaach."

He pulls up a chair and sits down close to me. There's a look of exhaustion across his lined face. He points to Pergo and asks, "You're one of Dan's patients, right?"

How's he know me?

"Yes, I am. Why do you call him that? Is it some sort of a nickname for Delaano?"

"Kind of. It's short for Dante...Dante Delano Pergo."

"Are you his fathaa?"

He looks at the bed. "No...no, not biologically...but he's as much of a son to me as there ever could be. His father named him after his favorite poet, Dante Alighieri. The middle after his favorite president. I always enjoyed it when Dan talked about his childhood. He loved to tell us about how he and his father would read the *Divine Comedy* together."

"Us?"

"Yeah, he'd discuss it with me and my daughter."

"Wow. That sounds like pretty intense stuff, especially for a kid."

"I know. That's what I always thought. His dad apparently loved literature. He told us how they would talk for hours about books and philosophy."

"No wonder Pergo is so smaart. This whole thing is so terrible, isn't it?"

"Yeah, I spent the night with him. I didn't think he would even make it to this morning. I was so shocked to get the call...I'm still not even sure what happened. His car was completely totaled." He pinches the bridge of his nose with one hand and massages his neck with the other. He looks so tired.

He nods at me. "I'm glad you came over to visit. I know it means a lot to him. I'm sorry...I apologize for bending your ear, son. I just talk too much when I get nervous."

"Oh, theaa's no reason to apologize. I'm glad to talk with ya. I was feelin' so bummed just sittin' here...so, how'd you know I was one of his paatients?"

"He used to talk with me about you...even though he wasn't supposed to. I guess he tried to pick my brain about your thinking because I'm a painter too."

"Huh, really? What kind of paintaa?"

"I'm an impressionist. I dabble with abstractions a little too. You see, Dan was...is involved with my daughter... but now."

"Pergo told me he was divorced. Was your daaughtaa his wife or...?"

"No, they never got the chance...to..." He breaks down. I feel like he might need some time alone, so I go out into the hallway and sit by the elevators. I figure he might need a drink, so I go to the vendin' machine and get 'im a cold OJ. When I come back in, he's reading somethin' aloud.

"*What no eye has seen, nor ear heard, nor heart of man imagined, what God has prepared for those who love him.* Hey, you're back, huh?"

"Yeah, I was just sitting outside. Heaa, I got ya a drink."

"That's very kind. Thank you." He cracks the cap and takes a big swig. "I'm just trying to read to him. You know, when people are like this they can still hear."

"Yeah, I learned about that this mornin'."

"I thought one of these gospels may help my boy here feel at peace."

Oh sure. Read the parts on if ya don't measaa up...how you'll suffaa eternally. That'll make him feel bettaa too.

I can't listen. "Hey, umm Levy. I'm gonna go home for a while. I'll be back in a few. Will I see you when I get back?"

"I'm not going anywhere," he replies with conviction. "See you later."

I tell the nurses to page Dr. Swanson. I explain that I'm going to take a walk to clear my head. She's pleased that

I'm handling this well—whatever that means. She explains a little more about the crash and tells me to call 'er if I need anythin'. I tell 'er I'm fine. I don't think she believes me though.

As I walk home, it starts to fuckin' rain. Some say raindrops are tears from God, but I doubt God has enough conscience to cry. Even though I cut through the Fenway Garden to knock off some of the distance, I'm drenched by the time I get home. A hot shower makes me feel a little better though—the fresh scent of citrus soap and warm spray.

I dry off and call Megan. "Hi, it's me."

"Hi." She's laughin' at somethin'.

"Sounds like you're havin' a good time."

"Yeah, I'm just watching Jay Leno's monologue from last night's *Tonight Show*. My parents taped it for me. They still use a VCR, if you can believe..."

I cut 'er off. "My friend was in a caar aaccident."

"Oh, my goodness, are they all right?" Her voice trembles.

"I don't know. He has a lot of brain traama."

"That's terrible. I was starting to get worried about you because I've been trying to call. I'm so sorry. Are you all right?"

"Yeah, I've been at the hospital with him. It's my friend, Delaano Pergo."

"What happened?"

"I don't know. It seems like a strange story. Apparently, he was drivin' wicked faast in the middle of the night. His caar...raammed into the side of a big tree on Storrow...there weren't even any skid maarks. I think he's going to..."

After a long period of silence, "I'm going to jump on the next train."

"No, wait. I'm all right. Look, I'll caall you once this gets bettaa sorted out. I'm going to go back ovaa to spend some more time with him. I just wanted to let you know what is goin' on. We'll talk soon, OK?"

"All right. But be sure to call me. In the meantime, I will pray for you both."

I take a cab back to the hospital. Even though the driver has his windshield wipers on high, you could barely see the road. Every so often, we would see a streak of wicked lightnin' in the sky. Then a boom of thunder would shake the car. The day really sucks so far.

When I get back to his room, Levy's still next to his bed readin' the frickin' Bible. When he notices me: "Hey there, young man. You look a lot better now that you showered."

"Yeah, I've heard that before. Did anythin' change?"

"Unfortunately, not...he's...he's just there in that vegetative state." His voice is hoarse and heavy. "Bad storm out there, huh?"

"You have no ideaa."

Our conversation bounces off the walls with a hauntin' echo. Within the blindin' paleness of the room, I notice a hint of color on the night table next to Pergo's bed. It's a small red dot on a framed Polaroid. It seems strategically placed to face Pergo's head. I don't remember seeing it there earlier, which makes me curious, so I get up to get a closer look. I pick up the frame and study it for a few. It's the picture from Pergo's office—the young woman in a red sweatshirt, standing next to a white van.

"That's my daughter...Chiara," he says.

"She's a knockout." I set the picture back on the table.

He doesn't respond. Instead, he just tenses his lips with a stoic acceptance of my words. He glances back at the picture, gets up, and repositions it back to its original position. Gingerly, he sets the frame down to be sure it's in the right spot. He swipes the side of his eye with his little finger as he completes the exercise.

Before he sits back down in his chair, a nurse enters the room and says, "Mr. Dawson, there is a telephone call for you at the nurses' station." Levy slowly follows her out of the room.

He returns a couple of minutes later and stands near the wall before repositioning his chair backward, where he straddles it like a cowboy on a thick-shouldered bull. He rests his elbows on the top and leans forward. He looks at me as if he wants to talk some more.

I say, "I think Delaano used to keep that photo in his office." I point to it.

He shakes his head in an affirmative direction. "Yes, that picture means a lot to him. God, this is all so difficult. Son, why don't we go grab some coffee and talk. I need to get out of this room. I'm going crazy."

"Yeah, me too. Appaarently, there's a coffee shop downstairs."

"Downstairs it is."

We descend a few floors on a cramped elevator towards the tiny self-serve shop with black and white floor tiles. We fill our cardboard cups with French roast and don't leave any room for cream. Levy pays the tab after we stand in a short line of blue and green-clad health care workers—tired souls attemptin' to rejuvenate. We find a table toward the corner and pour packets of sugar into our cups. It does nothin' to lessen the bitterness.

While waitin' for Levy to settle, I cradle the cup with my bent, rounded hands. The heat feels nice against my palms and fingers. I have so many questions, but he seems to need some time. He finally gets himself together after blowin' over his coffee, causing a tiny cloud of steam to fog his round, John Lennon-like glasses.

"It seems like you know Delaano a long time," I say.

"Yeah. Decades." He pauses, seemingly wonderin' where to start. He takes a small sip from his cup and purses his lips. "So, Zach, did you know that Dan was a professor early in his career? He was in the philosophy-psychology field."

"Huh. No, I didn't. He nevaa mentioned that."

"Yeah, he was a really big deal. Very famous with books and whatnot. But that all changed after...after the incident." He repositions his glasses.

"Wait, what incident...what are you talkin' about?"

"Chiara and her mother...my ex...they umm, had a...they had a terrible thing happen to...it changed our lives forever..."

"Event? I'm sorry, I'm not following, Levy." His posture tenses. He looks like he's in pain. "Sorry, I mean...this sounds so personal. You don't have to tell me...about any..."

He wipes his leaky nose and dabs his eyes with the corner of the brown, recycled napkin he used to carry his coffee over to the table. He slightly regains his composure and ignores my suggestion. "Well, you see, Dan met Chiara twenty years ago when she was a graduate student up here at BU. They fell for each other fast. At first, I was a little concerned since Dan was in his early forties and my girl was only twenty-six. I just wanted what was best for her, you know. Then I met Dan...such a nice guy...and I knew right off, they were meant for one another. They were even planning on getting married." He pauses and adds another packet of sugar into his cup. "Then, I don't know what happened, you see...Chiara went to reconnect with her mother, who...well, she hadn't seen for a long time. Then she and her mother were involved in this attack. It was in Mexico. It..."

I cut in without letting him go on. "Wait, what kind of attack? Is she OK?"

"Not really. None of us are...I'm sorry, son...let me pull myself together here." He stirs his coffee.

"It's aalright. Really you don't have..."

"See, it all happened when they were returning to their hotel from visiting the Mayan ruins in Tulum. They took this tour...which was like, I don't know...a trap...the ride home and everything. The tour van they were on pulled off the main road...it was barren. The driver told everyone that something seemed wrong with the transmission, that he wanted to look under the hood. That's what my ex said anyway. She said that at first, it seemed normal enough, but then...the driver told the group to stand outside while he looked under the hood. When Chiara and her mother stepped outside, they heard these commands from...this gang...four of them—ordering everyone to the ground... two with guns."

"Oh, my God. This is terrible."

"Yeah, and...then...the pricks collected everyone's stuff—purses, wallets, watches. They could have just left with the valuables, you know. But no...instead, the biggest son-of-a-bitch, dressed-up in military-style fatigues and a black tank, swung into action. He wasn't happy with just robbery...no, the scum wanted to steal some humanity as well. He apparently yelled 'Tu tan caliente,' before grabbing a young woman from the tour. He pointed a gun to her head and forced her behind some trees. His friends...chuckled and told him to hurry. Even though their noses were in the ground, everyone said the dry air smelled of liquor." Levy was red-faced and almost in a trance.

"You...don't have to...finish, Levy. Really..."

In a louder voice, "When Chiara's mother heard the girl's screams, she kicked one of the bastards in the balls and ran towards her. That's when she found the girl lying on the ground, unconscious...her clothes torn off and strewn among the stones. The scum tried to react...but was too surprised. See, the stupid fuck left his gun on one of the rocks when he was...rap...raping this young woman. When Chiara's mother found it, she placed the barrel at his ugly forehead, and...when he attempted to pull his pants up. She..." Levy sits higher in his chair. "I guess he thought he would get out of the situation. His absent look, his sickness, his perversion, his arrogance, his, his, his...they all dared her trembling hand. Arrogant bastard. She told me after, she heard the rest of them coming...the footsteps...that amid him spitting dark yellow phlegm from between his front teeth...she...sq...squeezed the trigger. By the time the rest of the pack arrived, they found their brother at the losing end of the gun. 'Hermano, Hermano,' they screamed when they saw his forehead blown into small pieces all over the ground. I love to think about how his head dissolved into shatters of bone, sinew, and brain, organically spread across the harsh landscape. Imagine painting it—the universal justice of cadmium red and scarlet splatters on ochre ground...his frontal lobe sagging like jelly into the crumbling dust." He sips from his coffee and is almost smiling. "You know, the frontal lobe is the part of the brain involved in decision making and planning. Huh, isn't it ironic—that's where she shot him? I was told that it glistened from the rays of the setting sun, igniting the shiny myelin." He relished this part of the story. His eyes dart around the coffee shop like he's dreamin'.

I feel itchy.

He goes on. "Yeah, Chiara's mother told me what happened after she...recovered."

"Recovaaed from what?"

"Well, that's where it gets complicated. After they saw their buddy on the ground...one of the thugs tackled my ex and started to choke her. She remembers bits and pieces...trying to breathe...then a loud bang...a burning sensation in her leg."

"Wait, they shot her?"

"No, apparently Chiara did."

"What...why would...?

"Well, after the first shot, people were scattering everywhere, including the thugs. Chiara went running to find her mom and apparently found the son-of-a-bitch choking her. She must have picked up the gun...fired a few shots at him. I guess she accidently hit her mom. That's what one of the guys on the tour thinks happened, because he said by the time he got there, he saw Chiara dropping the gun to the ground as she was running towards her mother. He said her mother was losing a lot of blood, and Chiara literally tried to stop the bleeding by wrapping her entire body around the wound."

"Holy shit."

"They had to pry her away so they could get them back to the van. They called the police...got them to a hospital. Chiara doesn't seem to remember much...she had shock or PTSD or something."

"What about the guy?"

"A couple of people told the police that they saw him limp off into the foothills with the help of another guy. Dan received the call from the police...then he called me. We were in Mexico fifteen hours later. Chiara gave the police Dan's business card...she had it in her bag...she was too broken up to call herself.

When Dan and I got to my ex's room, she was a mess. It was all so touch and go. Chiara was shivering...just shivering...sitting next to her mother's bed. When she saw us, she fell into our arms for what seemed like hours."

"It's OK, Levy." I lean over and pat him on the shoulder.

"I never would have made it through that time without Dan. He was back and forth between the states and Chiara's mother's bedside so many times during the first month. It's like he never slept."

"What happened to...?"

After a long-exaggerated pause, "Chiara's mother has almost fully recovered, except for a small limp. The bullet hit a big blood vessel and a nerve near her right knee. I mean it took a long time...years. You see, after a few weeks of being hospitalized in Mexico, she had very little movement in that leg. The doctors thought she would do better if she were transferred to a facility in the U.S. So, we made arrangements and flew her here to Boston...all the experts and everything. After months of therapy, we decided to take her home from the hospital. She still needed a lot of care...everything was so expensive, and she didn't even have insurance."

"What about Chiaara?"

"Well, that's the other part. Ever since that day, she hasn't been the same. Her whole personality has changed. She has major anxiety...barely leaves the house. She stays with her mother constantly...absolutely afraid to leave her. I mean, Dan saw all of this. That's when he decided to quit his professorship and start a private practice to make more money. Apparently, universities don't pay well. See, he paid for Chiara's mother's care with all the proceeds from his books. Even though he made a lot from them, especially after he appeared on Phil Donahue, he still needed a bigger salary. That's when he started his practice."

"I'm just not following, Levy. I knew that Dr. Pergo earned his Ph.D., but he nevaa mentioned the professaa part."

"Yeah, like I said he was a philosopher and a psychologist. I can't believe he didn't have you read any of his books."

"No, we nevaa...I didn't know..."

"Well, you should, they are someth... Anyway, Dan knew that Chiara's emotional trauma was an attempt to shut out the world. He knew to help her and her mother, he had to take drastic therapeutic actions. Christ, I can't believe how long all of this has gone on."

I ask, "Where's Chiaara now?"

"I haven't told her about any of this yet. I really don't know what to say...I'm afraid it will set her back...she's still so fragile. See, when this all happened, I moved here and got an apartment in Dan's building, right next to him, in fact. I live there with my ex and Chiara now. We all just kind of take care of one another...kind of like a team. As I said, Chiara doesn't like to leave the house much. Now with this, on top of everything else, I'm not sure she'll be able to handle it.

~~~

Dante

Paolo's phone rings. Its 11:35 PM, and he's not happy being interrupted from Johnny Carson's monologue. "Yes, ahh...who is it?"

"Paolo, It's Dan."

"Oh, Dan...I'm ahh sorry. I thought this would be a prank call at this ahh time of night. I heard what happened. Is she all right? I tried calling you, but I guess you haven't been home ahh."

"Yeah, I've been in Mexico. I just got back a few hours ago. Yes, thanks...she's physically stable. Her emotional health is a whole different story. She's still in Mexico with her mom and dad. I needed to get a few things settled here. I'm headed back in three days."

"My God. Those animals. I'm so sorry ahh...for all of this pain. How's her mother?"

"Doing better. She's stabilized. The wound is a bad one though."

"Thank ahh God that she's OK. What about the other girl?"

"They released her from the hospital the other day. Her fiancé came to take her home. The poor thing was doing all right. The fiancé was so grateful to Chiara's mom
~~~

for helping her. We all exchanged contact info so we can stay in touch."

"Well, I pray she gets back ahh to normal."

"Yes...prayers...any positive energy would be helpful. Paolo, do you recall the part of my book where I discuss limiting the influence of toxic vessels?"

"Yes, of course, I remember that part. I greatly agree with your points on this ahh."

"Well, I need some help from some of your North End colleagues. I would like to reduce the number of toxic vessels in this world."

"I understand. But for this, I must ahh call you in the morning, please. Is that OK?"

"Perfect. Talk then." They hang up.

Dan goes over to his safe and dials in the combination, Chiara's phone number. He reaches inside for his cash. He pulls out a briefcase and flicks through the bills—seventy-five thousand dollars. He'd been saving proceeds from his book for a rainy day, and now, it was pouring. He places the briefcase on his table and falls asleep. At 7 AM, the phone rings. "Dan ahh...I have scheduled a meeting this morning with a few people who can help with the vessels. Can you meet us at T's café at nine?"

"I'll be there at eight-thirty."

He's having an expresso when they come in. Three men follow Paolo like a group of soldiers.

"Dan ahh, you remember...Tony?"

"Hey there, Dan." They shake. "You still got that grip, huh? I'm sorry to hear about your situation."

"Hello, Tony...thanks...thanks for coming."

"My pleasure. Dan, I want to introduce you to my cousins—Rocco and Vanni."

"Hello. Nice to meet you."

"The pleasure is ours, Dante. Any friend of Paolo's is a friend of ours," says Rocco.

Tony goes to the counter and orders expressos for the table. While he waits, he kids around with the barista, a shapely woman with red hair and big breasts. She stacks the cups on a tray, and Tony carries them to the table. He sits. "I got the coffee, but she still won't give me her number. What a hard nut to crack." Tony looks her way and blows a kiss. She smiles and gives him a fingertip wave. He refocuses his attention to the table. "Dan, maybe you can explain your situation to the boys."

After a brief overview, Dan gets to the point. "Well guys, when there is a tumor inside the body, it must be removed...right?"

"Yes, Dante. I believe so," says Vanni.

"Well, I need your help with a surgery. There are a few tumors south of the border that need to be resected."

"That's what we do. Boston has some of the greatest surgeons in the world," says Tony.

"This I know. My request may be a little unique though. You see, I would like to do this surgery myself. I just need some extra hands to make sure the procedure goes smoothly."

Paolo asks, "But Dan ahh, you have never done this sort of thing before. Wouldn't it be easier to have an experienced team take ahh care of these ills?"

"No. If there's blood, I want it on my own hands." His tone is ice. His gaze unyielding.

Tony glances at his cousins. They nod. Tony asks, "Do we have the operating room scheduled?"

"I'm going back down there in a few days. I have a few

leads on the patients, where they live and everything. It was easy to get the information from the funeral posting. You know, from the fuck that Chiara's mother shot."

"Well, we are flexible. But why not just let the police take care of this?"

"I don't trust them. I think they're protecting these guys. I can't let them just walk free...ya know? Why don't I buy three tickets for next week? I can pick you up at the airport when you get down there." He hands Tony the briefcase. "Do you think this will cover your efforts?"

Tony gets up from the table. "Excuse me, gentlemen. I need to use the restroom." A few minutes later, he comes back to the table and says, "Gentlemen, I'm hungry for some tacos, interested in joinin' me?"

~~~

Zach

After Levy and I exchange phone numbers, I leave the hospital for the day. I'm exhausted and overwhelmed when I get home. I call Megan and update her on everythin'. I also start to tell her about me—even how I met Pergo and all. We talk for hours. Pergo was right, she did handle it well, and despite the mess I am, she still arrives the next morning. After tightly embracin' on the South Station platform, I grab her heavy overnight bag and sling it over my shoulder. We hold hands on the way to the truck.

"Thank you for coming," I say.

"You don't need to thank me. I wanted to be here for you. This is so horrible. I feel terrible, for you...for everyone."
~~~

"It means a lot. Would you mind if we stopped at the hospital on our way home? I want to check in with Levy and all."

"Of course, I don't mind." She plays with the curls on the back of my head as we drive.

"So, how was the train ride?"

"It was OK. The drive to Brunswick was easy and the train was pretty fast. The woman sitting next to me on the train was so loud though. I had to find another seat to read. She was talking with her girlfriend about such banal topics. She had this entitled, annoying voice. Like it reminded me of women that live a little west of Philadelphia—they call it the Main Line or something."

"I've never been to Philadelphia. I heard they have a great aart museum theaa."

"Yeah, great restaurants too."

"Well, here's the hospital. Let's see where we can paark." I pull into the underground garage. "We can just lock your stuff up in the baack. It'll be safe."

"I'm not worried."

When we get to Pergo's room, Levy graciously stands up from his chair. "Well, hello."

"Levy, this is Megaan."

"I'm so glad to meet you, honey. I understand this guy is crazy about you," he says.

Not the best choice of words, Levy.

The atmosphere is the same as yesterday. The monitors are blinkin' and everythin' seems so bleak. Megan takes a long glance at Pergo. I can see her whisperin' a prayer under her breath before studying the monitors.

"How's it look? She was a pre-med major in school," I

explain to Levy.

"It's hard to tell much from this. They are just his vital signs. His blood pressure is very high though."

"The doctor was in here a little earlier today; he thought things were looking the same as before. The head trauma started a severe hemorrhage on the brain, they drained some of the fluid, but the pressure in his skull is still excessively high. We can't do much here. Come on, let's get a snack or something. You must be hungry, Megan."

"I am a little. I mean if you both want to eat something, too."

We go to the coffee shop and buy a gigantic cinnamon bun. We slice it into threes. I look up at Levy. He's chowin' on his third, like he hasn't eaten in days.

After a few minutes, Megan says, "I understand you are very close to Dan. I am really sorry for all that you are going through." I know she's talkin' to me too.

Levy responds, "Dan is a son to me." After he clears his throat, "He's in love with my daughter...Chiara. You remind me a lot of her, you know...when she was your age."

"Thank you. That is such a beautiful compliment."

"You're welcome, honey. Maybe you will get a chance to meet her someday. I brought her here earlier, but I had to bring her right back home. She isn't taking this well." His eyes are swollen with huge, bluish-purple circles.

"Are you doing OK, Levy?"

"Yeah, I'm all right. The Lord doesn't give us any more than we can handle, right?"

"That's the truth," says Megan.

"I just worry about Chiara. God, I hate seeing her

hurt." He pauses. "Let's' just try to think of something positive." Another pause. "So, what are you kids going to do today?"

"Well, I think I'm going to take Megaan ovaa to the MFA aftaa we leave heaa. Then we're gonna hit Newbury and then maybe the public gaarden."

"That sounds nice. It's a great day for that."

"Would you like to join us?"

"No, thank you, honey. I am going to stay here for a bit. Then I should get back home. I have a bunch of things to take care of. I mean, I have to see how my girl is."

"Levy, we are glad to help in any way we can."

"Thanks. I promise to let you know if I need anything. For now, there's not much you kids can do. Why don't you get over to the museum? I'll call you if anything changes." We reluctantly agree, and Megan hugs Levy goodbye with the vigor of a newly adopted daughter.

We spend the day as planned. Between the museum and the public garden, we walk miles. After a ride on a Swan Boat, we find a bench to sit and talk.

"You must think I'm a nut," I say.

"No, I don't. I'm a pretty good judge of character. After we talked, I did a deep dive on you over the internet. I got to read some articles and watch some news clips. I don't think you did anything wrong. I mean, I don't like your paintings of the president on the cross, or the last supper...for me, they're kind of sacrilegious. But I respect your artistic right to portray your feelings. I don't think it's been easy for you, being a foster child and all."

"It hasn't. I don't want you to feel sorry for me, though. I think I'm comin' out of it all...you know, a little bit ahead." I smile at her. She leans in and kisses me.

"Come on, I'll cook you dinner, 'Vincent.' You have any pasta?"

"Huh, if I had an ounce of van Gogh's talent, you'd be talkin' to my agent instead of me. Ha, ha. Yeah, I probably a have couplaa boxes of spaghetti, but you don't haveta cook, we can..."

"No, I want to. All right?"

"Thank you. That will be nice."

When we arrive at my apartment, she comments about how clean and organized everythin' is. We talk about my condition and stuff, but I don't mention the monsignor.

She makes linguini with olive oil, black pepper, garlic, and Romano. We eat almost the whole pound, and dip chunks of Italian bread along the bottom of our bowls. After dinner, we move over to the couch, where she falls asleep, her gorgeous head resting on my shoulder. I wrap her with a small blanket while admiring her innocence. I'm not far behind and doze off shortly after. She wakes and kisses me. Her lips feel soft and warm. She straddles my lap...we're breathing heavy. It feels so...until the phone rings. It's Levy.

I hear his matter-of-fact tone. "OK. Yes. We'll be ovaa in a few. Yes, I'm aalright. Thanks," I say.

I set the receiver down and don't need to explain. Like newspaper print, she reads the black message on the paleness of my face. She reaches for my arm and holds me. She guides me up and takes my head to her shoulder.

"Come on, let's get your jacket on and go over to the hospital. I'll drive, all right?" My ears are hummin' like a thousand cicadas.

It's difficult to make things stick. When glue dries, it

crumbles and flakes. The bonds between the surfaces open up and barren crevasses are exposed. Climbaas lose their footin' in these kinda' holes, slippin' between, and then holdin' on to the crusted remains for deaar life. Liftin' one out of the cold depths requires a partnaa. How'd I make it this faar without one?

When we get there, Levy is finishing some paperwork with the medical staff. When he sees us, he pauses his business and hugs us. After a few apologies, and directions for the next steps from a team of nurses, Levy leans back and explains that Pergo wanted to be cremated. He also tells us that he wants to host a memorial service for Pergo's friends.

Megan asks, "Doesn't he have any other family?"

"None that he's close with. His parents died years ago."

"What can we do?"

"I guess I could use some muscle sorting out his apartment. Maybe after the service. I'll call you and update you on the plans. Right now, I just need to go home and tell Chiara and her mother the news."

~~~

Dante

Dan returns to Mexico. He rents a car and drives directly to the hospital, where he meets Levy and Chiara in the early evening. They greet each other with hugs and kisses. Chiara's mother is asleep. In a hopeful voice: "Hi guys, any change?"

"Yes, she's doing much better," says Levy.

"Oh, that's good. Honey, how are you?" Chiara doesn't answer. Instead, she just tucks her head into his shoulder.
~~~

He kisses her hair. "Has the care been all right? What have the doctors said?"

Levy says, "The muscle damage is pretty severe. They are not sure about the neurological elements either. They think if we could get her back to the states, we could think about therapy and whatnot."

"Then that's what we should do."

Chiara asks, "How was your trip?"

"It was a bumpy ride, but overall...fine. I got a lot of my business situated at home."

"Well, that's good."

"Hey, I bet you both need a break. Why not let me sit with her tonight?"

"Thanks. It has been a long day. We could use some rest. Are you sure you don't mind? Will you call us if anything changes?"

"Of course. I won't hesitate."

"OK. See you in the AM." They hug goodbye.

On their way out, Dan says, "Hey Levy, I think when we do move her, we should go to Boston. I contacted one of my surgeon friends. He told me there's several therapeutic strategies to help her regain function in that leg."

"I'm glad to go wherever the best care is."

"Oh, and Levy, did the police say anything more?"

"No. They just told us they are continuing the investigation."

"All right. Goodnight." They shuffle out.

Dan pulls a chair close to Chiara's mother. He leans forward near her still head. Softly, he whispers, "I'm so sorry you are going through this. If only I hadn't suggested...maybe this could have been..." He leans back.

Minutes pass. "It must be weird...I mean maybe even nice...being all together again...despite...You know, Levy and Chiara are by your side every day. You have to come out of this...I mean Chiara needs to see that you're all right. I promise there's more justice to be had for those scum balls...but...for now, just focus on getting well."

***

Levy and Chiara return early the next morning. Chiara hugs and kisses her mom. Levy asks, "How is she? Did you get any sleep?"

"She's just quiet. Kind of in and out of a deep dream. Yeah, I dozed off in the chair."

"That's no good. Why don't you go get some rest back at the hotel? We'll stay with her now," says Chiara.

"Sounds good. I have a few errands that I want to take care of first though. Be back later. You don't want to go, do you?"

Chiara says, "No, you go ahead. I just want to stay...with mo..."

"OK. I won't be long. Give me a hug. See you in a bit."

Dan buys a local map at a tourist shop. He pulls out the folded newspaper page with the funeral notice of Jorge Martinez and locates his address on the map. He suspects he'll find some of the other guys at the same location. He drives to the outskirts of town and locates a small shack matching the address. He sits in his car and sees an older woman, dressed in black, sitting on a broken rocking chair, watching two little boys playing hockey with sticks and a crushed aluminum can. He wonders who she is...who the boys are. He also doesn't want to be noticed, so he drives around the block and parks at a small tienda.

About half an hour later, he drives by the shack again. Now, two young men are on the porch drinking beers. He parks across the street and watches them for about twenty minutes. One of them has a limp. Using Chiara's camera, he shoots some photographs. He drives back to the hospital.

It's mid-afternoon and oppressively hot. His shirt is soaked with sweat. When he enters, Levy and Chiara are talking at a small table in the corner of her mother's room.

"You look like you ran over here," says Chiara.

"Man, it's a hot one today. How are things?"

"We're all right...get your errands done?"

"Yeah, I did...had to make some calls to my publi...Hey, I stopped off at the police station to see if they had made any progress." He reaches into his pocket and pulls out the Polaroids. "The police asked me to see if you recognized these two guys." He shows Chiara the pictures. She studies their slim bodies, tattoos, and long, jet-black hair.

"Oh, my God, that's them. I'll never forget their faces. And that tattoo. See the Jaguar?" Her face tenses.

"OK, good. I'll tell the police that they may be on to something," he says with a callous affect.

After a pause: "Dan, can I talk with you in the hall?"

"Sure." They walk out of the room. "What's up?"

"I know those photos are from my camera. You need to promise you won't...do..."

"Do wha...?" She stops him with her finger at his lip.

"Just stop. OK?"

"Don't you think there's a price to pay? They should burn in hell."

"We all should," she says before going back inside the room.

~~~

Zach

His service is fittingly bein' held today, a week before Labor Day. We're sayin' goodbye to him and summaa all at the same time. I take a break from gettin' ready and step outside into the still air. I sit on my stoop and inventory the street. Town is crowded with college kids movin' into their apartments. U-Hauls are double-parked all over the road. I see a couple of parents huggin' their daughter goodbye. It looks like they moved her in next door. The frickin' dad's sobbin'.

"Hey, to all you guys out theaa. How's it goin for ya? Good...good. You see, all I wanna say is that the similarity of sayin' goodbye to someone alive or dead is hope. When they're alive, you hope you'll see 'em soon. When they're dead, you hope they find heaven and maybe you'll catch up with 'em lataa or somethin'. I mean if ya don't believe in heaven, ya really don't have any hope...'specially when shit like this happens. You don't have any delusions eithaa, but no mattaa...the whole thing just kinda sucks. Any thoughts?"

I go back inside. Megan's just showered and is dabbin' some musk behind her ears. She's dressed nice—a knee-length, black dress. Her hair is tightly pulled back with a thick elastic band. She asks if I'm ready to go.

"Almost, just let me finish gettin' dressed." The truth is, I'm not. I'm just delayin'...If I could only turn back the clock.
~~~

We take a cab to the North End. Levy's got this whole life celebration thing planned, and from what he explained, Pergo's good friend, Paolo, was able to rent his church's community room. That's where we're gettin' dropped off. A f...in' church community room. I'm not sure if it'll be religious, and frankly, it doesn't matter to me. I'm just happy to be part of...ya know, the send-off. He was like a fath...shit, I can't talk about it anymore.

When we get out of the taxi, a long line is streamin' through the entrance. Standin' a few people ahead of me, I see Anna. She's wipin' the corners of her eyes with a tissue. We say hello to each other before goin' in.

It's quiet in the room and everyone's whisperin'. Me and Megan make it over to our seats—foldout chairs with red vinyl cushions. The air deflates when we sit on 'em. It makes a pretty loud noise. I feel a little embarrassed because I don't want anyone to think it was a fart or anythin'.

I don't usually wear a jacket and tie, but I wanted to show Pergo that, ya know, I've got nothin' but respect for him. I mean, that's the kind of stuff he deserves. I see Levy in the front of the room. Next to him is a woman in a plain lookin' navy dress. It looks like Chiara...from the picture and all. Next to her is a fit, older woman with a noticeable limp. Must be his ex. A few seats over, sits a stocky guy and a slim lady. Behind them is a row of handsome, impeccably dressed guys. Then there's a bunch of people all around that I've seen before in his waitin' room...a bunch of strangers too. A good lookin' woman on the end seems pretty broken up. Oh, there's Dr. Swanson. I point 'er out to Megan. Shit, the room is really packed.

The service starts with some acoustic guitar stuff,

which accordin' the little program they gave us at the door, is being done by Dr. Chelsea Berne. She plays that song Clapton wrote for his kid when he died. I can't remember the name of the song, but it makes Megan cry. After the music stops, Levy gets up and starts talkin'. "Good afternoon, everyone. Thank you for joining us to celebrate the special life of Dr. Dante Delano Pergo. While his passing has been difficult for all of us, I would like us to reflect on how he deeply touched our lives. He was such a special person, always there to help and support us. He has helped my family...or I should say, his family, in ways that are unimaginable. His essence lives on. This is from 1 Corinthians 15:53-55, '*For this perishable body must put on imperishability, and this mortal body must put on immortality. When this perishable body puts on imperishability, and this mortal body puts on immortality, then the saying that is written will be fulfilled. Death has been swallowed up in victory. Where, O death, is your victory? Where, O death, is your sting*?' God bless you, son. Rest in peace."

Next, the stocky guy from the front of the room gets up and introduces himself. "Good day ahh. My name ahh is Paolo Bettullio." He pauses. "Dan ahh, was like my brother. I've known him all ahh my adult life. We went through so much together. This is not the way I dreamed it..." He sniffles. "Anyway, ladies and gentleman, Dan ahh, loved Walt Whitman. His favorite work by him was *Song of Myself*. This is mmm from section twenty-five. Feel free to read along in the booklet. Please also, umm, note that I changed the name Walt to Dan as ahh indicated with the asterisk.

Dazzling and tremendous how quick the sun-rise would kill
me,
If I could not now and always send sun-rise out of me.

We also ascend dazzling and tremendous as the sun,
We found our own O my soul in the calm and cool of the day-
break.

My voice goes after what my eyes cannot reach,
With the twirl of my tongue I encompass worlds and volumes
of worlds.

Speech is the twin of my vision, it is unequal to measure itself,
It provokes me forever, it says sarcastically,
** Dan you contain enough, why don't you let it out then?*

Come now I will not be tantalized, you conceive too much of
articulation,
Do you not know O speech how the buds beneath you are
folded?
Waiting in gloom, protected by frost,
The dirt receding before my prophetical screams,

I underlying causes to balance them at last,
My knowledge my live parts, it keeping tally with the meaning
of all things,
Happiness, (which whoever hears me let him or her set out
in search of this day.)

My final merit I refuse you, I refuse putting from me what I
really am,
Encompass worlds, but never try to encompass me,
I crowd your sleekest and best by simply looking toward you.

Writing and talk do not prove me,
I carry the plenum of proof and every thing else in my face,
With the hush of my lips I wholly confound the skeptic.

"Let us have ahh, a moment of silence, please ahh."

Paolo then invites some of Dan's past students, Drs. Noah Apstein and Jason Haley, to say a few words. They walk to the front of the room and talk about how they never would have made it through graduate school without Delano's support. They tell us how they try to emulate Pergo with their own students now. They also say something about his generous vessel, but it sounds a little stupid. I'm not sure what they mean.

Things get quiet and Chiara stands before the group. She wipes her eyes and her quiverin', pink mouth. "Thank you all for coming today. I know Dan is...looking down on us, with pride...I mean he was proud of his friends and students. I'm not sure I have words for how broken...I...we feel without hi...I mean he saved me from...well, like I said words can't...Dan, just know that we miss you more than...I just love you beyond any of this... God, let him rest in peace." She falls back into her chair and deteriorates into a puddle of tears. Levy and her mother try to comfort her. It doesn't really work.

Everything is quiet, except for Chiara cryin'. That is 'till the endin' song gets goin'—Ave Maria. At first, Dr. Berne was too broken up to sing it, but when she finally does, she belts it out. What a voice. She's kinda hot too.

After all that, we move to another room set up with round tables. People are dartin' in and out of the little bathroom, while others go to the tiny bar to order drinks. There's a big caterin' table in the front. It has a huge red, white, and green banner with *The Daily Catch* written across the front.

Dr. Bettullio offers a toast with his Chianti, "Let's raise our glasses to our friend ahh, Dr. Dante Delano Pergo. He would have enjoyed this party. Let him have peace. Cin, cin..." The well-dressed guys echo his toast in deep voices. I splash some wine on the bottom of my white shirt with the toast. Megan tells me not to worry; she can get the stain out for me later.

We all serve ourselves. I chow on Caesar salad, calamari meatballs, lobster fra diavolo, and squid ink pasta. Megan eats the same stuff, except for the Caesar salad. Apparently, she doesn't like anchovies. I mean, she eats oysters but not anchovies. Who does that, huh? Still, she tells me she thinks it was one of the best catered meals she's ever eaten. I agree. (It's the only catered meal I've ever eaten. Ha, ha).

"Hey, to all you guys out theaa. So, you have a minute? I just want to tell you how weird the luncheon got aftaa that. First, I have to say, it was nice of Levy to invite me and Megaan to sit at his table. Ya know, it was initially uncomfortable, and we were kinda' quiet. But then after a few, we started to converse a little more. Megaan and Chiaraa seemed to like each othaa...everythin' was goin' fine. I mean, we were sad and everythin', but it was OK until about midway through. That's when the community room, or whatever it's fr...in' called, started to get wicked hot. So, I decided to take off my tie and loosen the top buttons of my shirt to cool off some. Me and Megaan, we were still talkin', you know, BSin' about art and everythin', until I started to get a little uncomfortable with Chiara's mothaa. She wouldn't stop lookin' at me...I mean really, at my neck and stuff...and every time she did, she seemed to cry even more than she did durin' the service. Chiaraa wasn't much affected durin' the luncheon. I guess she cried herself out earliaa. In between the few words she had with Megaan, Chiara just staared straight ahead in a sort of a depressed stupaa. So, I leaned over to Megaan and told her I wanted to go. She asked if I was OK. I just told her I wasn't feelin' good. She told me she'll handle it. I have to ask you, really...what would I do without 'er right now? I mean, she's such a kind person takin' care of me and everythin'. I want to tell her that I lo... Oh, nevaa mind. Now's not the time, right?"

After Levy comes back from going from table to table talkin' with the guests, Megan goes up to him in her classy way. "Levy, Zach isn't feeling well. I'm going to take him home. Sorry, we are leaving a little early. This was such a beautiful service. Thank you, and God bless your family."

"God bless you too, honey. Zach, this is a lot. Go get some air. It will make you feel better."

"Thanks. I'm OK. I just need to rest."

Megan follows, "Also we are glad to help with anything. Anything at all. OK?"

"Yes. Yes. I guess I could use a little muscle tomorrow, if you have a few hours. That's if Zach's feeling all right."

"I'm sure he'll be fine. Just tell us what time," Megan says.

"Why don't you meet me at our building, say noon? Here's the address."

"OK. Thanks again. Try to get some sleep."

"Ha, ha. I wouldn't know what to do with it, honey." They hug. We say goodbye to Chiara and her mom. Her mom's still lookin' at me all weird and everythin'. We take a cab back to my pad.

She asks, “Are you feeling OK?”

“Yeah, it was just too hot in there,” I say. “It was makin’ me feel claaustrophobic.”

~~~

Dante

"Tony, it’s me. Can you talk?"

"Of course, Doc. How’s Chiara and her ma’ doin’?"

"A little better. It’s so hard to see them like this though."

"So, you ready for us to fly down?”

“That’s what I’m calling about. The...umm...procedure is on hold. I don’t think I’ll need your help. You and the boys can keep the money and everything."

“No way. The money’s here when you get back. Put it to good use for your family, huh? I’ll tell the surgical team the patient recovaaed...Ha, ha. Are you doing OK?”

“Yes, I’m fine. Thank you. You’re a good friend.”

“Anything for you, Dan. Call me when you’re back in town. I’ll let Paolo know, too.”

“Thanks. I’ll see you soon.”

~~~

Zach

The next morning, we’re right on time. We ring the doorbell and Levy lets us in. He escorts us up a wide turn-of-the-century stairwell to Pergo’s pad. The wooden stairs are stained dark on the edges, with a strip of red carpet through the center. His place has a big wooden door with ornate designs along the frame. Levy opens it up and we shuffle in. Like his office, Pergo's place is decorated nicely. Almost every wall is clad with art—paintings and photographs. While I admire an interesting abstract series, the huge photo hangin' over the grand fireplace really catches my eye. It's a black and white of giant trees. At first, I thought it was Ansel Adams, but it's signed Dawson instead. On the mantle sits a big urn, with RIP Ellis, etched in the metal. Next to it, sits a framed script with a small picture of a dog enclosed by a glass cover. Megan looks over my shoulders and we read it togethaa.

> *I had a dog. He was a golden retriever. He was always cautious around stairs, because when he was a puppy, he fell down a few. He would jump in circles when I asked him for a walk. He loved pizza and Chinese food and drank milk with gentle slurping sounds. He was perfect. His broad shoulders were elegantly poised for hugs. His kisses were warm and wet and in great contrast to his pink, frosty nose. He slept with his back against the wall and snored in the middle of the night. He only had love for this world...for butterflies, dogs, squirrels, cats, and people...just unconditional love. He taught me what exists behind the blue-azure, purple clouds at sunset. I miss him every day. His legacy lives on at the trees he marked along the square. I keep his bowl in the kitchen, hoping he might come back sometime. His name was Ellis.*

"Huh, that's really nice," says Megan."

"Yeah, I love those big dogs," I say.

"Me too. Especially goldens...They're so smart."

"Levy comes into the room with masking tape and boxes. "You kids ready to do some packing?"

"Sure are."

"All right, let's load these books up then."

The bookshelves are filled. Pergo's place is like that bookstore up in Camden, except it doesn't stink. Among the hundreds of titles, I notice a few red journals stacked on the first shelf. I pick one up and glance inside. Most of the pages are empty, but a couple of 'em had some writin'—pencil with neat penmanship. It makes me curious.

I ask Levy, "Do you think it's aalright to look through this?"

"I don't see why not. Would you like to take it with you, son? This way you can look through it later, after we get our work done. Let's just get the rest of the books into...I mean, if we could get that one thing done today, we'll be in good shape." Levy and Megan go into the second bedroom to load some items.

As I set the red journal on the table, a yellowed newspaper clippin' falls from the middle pages to the floor. I bend over to retrieve it.

Bodies Recovered

TULUM (AP) – The charred bodies found by tourists near the Pit Cenote in Dos Ojos Natural Park were identified as those of the Martinez brothers, who went missing last Thursday. Antonio and José Luis Martinez, ages 19 and 23, were found bound and badly burned. Police are asking for the public's help in solving the case.

Just as I finish reading it, Levy comes back in the room. He asks, "What do you have there?"

"Just this newspapaa clippin'." I hand it to him. "It fell out of that red journal." I point to it.

Levy looks at the clipping and quickly folds it up into his pocket. "Dan must have been using it for a...a bookmark. I'll throw it away later."

"Yeah, probably."

I get to work. I load up about ten boxes of books, before I take a break. "Shit, my arms are sore. Pergo was a nut about books."

From the other side of the room, Levy says, "He was a huge reader. I have to get you some copies of the books he wrote too."

"I would like that...thanks. What's with all these Alan Watts books?"

"I'm not sure. I know he really liked him though."

"Where are these going?"

"His will indicates the whole collection go to the public schools."

"That's the perfect place for them," says Megan.

We finish the packing midway through the day. "I can't thank you kids enough for your help. The Salvation Army will pick up the furniture and other stuff next week. The school is sending some guys by tomorrow for these books. Honey, I know you are leaving tomorrow. I cannot tell you how much of a pleasure it was to meet you. Please stay in touch."

She hugs him for at least a minute and kisses his cheek. "I will always stay in touch with you. You will be in my prayers every day, too."

"Son, I'll call you. Maybe we'll do some painting together."

"I would really like that," I say.

We could hear the echo of his apartment door closing as we exit the building. When we get home, we exhaustedly sit on my couch and talk a little.

Megan says, "Wow, we've been through a lot in such a little time."

"I would say so. My head is spinnin'. I can't believe he's gone. I just don't know what I'm gonna do."

"Did Dr. Swanson say anything about it? You know. A plan."

"Yes, she said to call her next week and she'll help me find anothaa theraapist. But I don't like the idea of findin' someone new. He can't just be replaced."

"No, he can't, but you have to do what's best for you. See what she has to say; I'm sure she's working in your best interest."

"I guess. You want a glass of OJ?"

"That sounds good."

I get up and go to the kitchen. I briefly peer out the window and watch some boys playin' stickball in the alley. The one wearin' the Sox jersey is a good hitter. He's got a lot of power. The others suck.

I bring the OJ back into the living room and place it on my antique coffee table, the one I refinished with dark, walnut stain.

"You hungry?"

"Yeah, you wanna go out for a bite?"

"No, let's just stay here and eat the leftovers. I feel too tired to go out. We could just watch TV and chill."

I go back to the kitchen and microwave the leftover pasta. I also heat up two bowls of tomato soup, which is what I was in the mood for anyway. I set the bowls on a big tray and bring it over to the table. She says a prayer, thankin' God for the food. I want to tell 'er that I'm the one who heated it up, but I let it go. I rip off a piece of crusty bread and dab it in the soup. I burn the roof of my mouth and blow on the next spoonful.

"What would you like to watch?"

"Oh, I don't care. Let's check out the news."

I turn the television on and flip through the stations. The choices are few. We come across an interview with Cheney talkin' about foreign policy.

They called me unpatriotic...when this little fuck has carte de blanche for...FUCK HIM. Ya can't rewrite history, DICK. Ya should be in jail for war crimes.

"Can you flip the station? I can't watch this person," she says.

"Gladly, you already know how I feel about him. Of all the demonic themes I have laid out on my canvases, I find him to be the most difficult, 'cause I can nevaa graasp the correct tones for his cold skin. It's like a signaature ugliness that becomes biggaa every time he speaks."

"He is awfully pale."

"Yeah, I heard he has a bad heaart. I actually think he has no heaart, like the tin..." We giggle.

"Hey, keep that one on. I like the Hallmark Channel."

"Do we haveta?"

She says, "No, I don't care. I just thought some romance might be nice. I have to say, I really don't want to go back tomorrow. I wish I could just stay here. I have to make class though, so I should leave somewhat early. Are you all right driving me to the train station?" She slurps her soup.

"Of course. I wish your visit wasn't under these circumstances though."

"Me too. Next time it will be different."

"What did your mom say about all this? Was she maad that you came down heaa?"

"Yes, at first. You know Asian women are pretty conservative. I mean she even likes Cheney. But after I told her about what happened to your friend, she was supportive. She even asked me to invite you back to Camden. She said she and my father would like to meet you."

"Does she know about my paintings and stuff?

"I haven't explained that part yet. That's going to be a huge uphill discussion."

"What about us? Have you said anything about me to Nolaan?"

"No, I haven't. I'm still so confused, and I would want to tell him in person anyway." She pauses and eats a scoop of linguini, vacuuming up the last noodle. Can we just take this one day at a time?"

"Yes, of course. I can't thank you enough for being heaa for me."

"Maybe it was more for me?" She smiles.

She leaves the next day. I drop her off at the train station and watch her walk away with warmth in my heart. Her ass looks good too.

~~~

Dr. Dante Delano Pergo

After leaving Zach's apartment, Dr. Pergo goes to his office. While he is relieved that Zach's scan turned out negative, he remains concerned about his outburst. Listening to Zach on the phone also has Dr. Pergo reliving his
~~~

own demons in encouraging Chiara to visit her mother. And then there's the other stuff too. He sits for hours and thinks.

When he makes it home, he parks behind the apartment building and cleans out his glove compartment. Looking out towards the Cambridge side of the Charles, he studies a thin cloud cover that tightly holds its grip on the big setting sun. A Monarch butterfly brushes against his shoulder as he unlocks the back entrance. After slowly ascending the stairs to his flat, he changes into a new set of clothes and decides to do some journaling. When he finishes two entries, he sets his pencil down and places the journal on a bookshelf.

He goes next door to spend some time with Chiara. Chiara's mom is out, and Levy is watching TV. Levy greets him. "Hey there. You look beat. How's Zach?"

"He's a bit of a mess, Levy. I don't know if he is ever going to be able to appropriately deal with his issues. Huh, for that matter, I'm not sure I can appropriately deal with mine either. Ha, ha."

"We're all a little nuts around here, aren't we? Hey, she's in her room. You hungry? There's leftovers in the fridge."

"No thanks. I'm good. Let me go see her. I missed her a lot today. Was it a good day?"

"Yes. We had a good day."

Dan taps on the door before entering. She's asleep with some music on. He doesn't want to wake her and gently kisses her head before whispering, "Hi honey, how are you? I'm sorry I wasn't around much the last two days. I was working with Zach; he had some big issues with this girl he has fallen for. You know, a therapist's job is never done. You look nice today. Do you want me to lower the air conditioning? It feels cold in here." He places a blanket over her.

He crawls into bed, carefully trying not to shake the mattress in the process. He holds her full-armed. In a whisper, "Chiara, I...I just wish I could change everything...for you...your parents...for me. For so long...I am just so...sor...honey. I want you to know that you've brought me so much...You are so stro...I can't...I love you."

She doesn't stir.

With that, he kisses her forehead before leaving the apartment. Levy is now snoozing on the couch. Dan looks at him kindly and locks the door behind him, double-checking to make sure it's secure.

~~~

Zach

"Hey, to all you guys out theaa. It's' been a long time since we talked. Can you believe it's been over a year since Pergo passed? I miss him. I was a bettaa person when he was around. I gotta tell ya, I think about him a lot, particularly when I look at the paintings Levy gave me from his office. I also think about him when I read that journal I took. I keep it on my nightstand. I don't let any of the othaas touch it though. It's mine.

"I don't really have many visitors. Mostly, only Levy and Chiara's mom. In fact, she comes to see me a couplaa times a week and usually brings me cookies. I don't know why she's so dedicated to me. Shit, I barely know 'er. She's always askin' me a bunch of questions about my childhood and stuff.
~~~

"One day she came in heaa with Levy. He told me he went to Muir woods and sprinkled Pergo's and Ellis's aashes undaa some of those big trees. Levy said that Pergo wanted it that way. Levy also told me that he thought I should go paint theaa sometime, the light and everythin'.

"Bein' in this environment has really helped me think. Lately, I have been ponderin' evolution. The idea of survival of the fittest makes a lot of sense to me. I'm not sure though, whethaa we all descended from one common aancestor. I think biologists overstate their theories sometimes. I also think a lot about God, that eternal primordial singulaa bein' who supposedly created the heaavens and the eaarth. I mean, since you can't make somethin' from nothin', where did all the universal ingredients come from? Megaan got me hooked on all this nonsense. It really makes me itch.

"Megaan's answaa is, 'The problem has less to do with the believability of God than it does with the concept of time. Time is a human convention. The renewal, cyclical nature of days and nights, the orbits of planets, the seasons. That's where it was derived. It's just a way for us to think about change.' Megaan tells me I don't deal well with change. So anyway, she said, 'If we take out the artificial constraint of time out of our thinking, then the existence of God is easier to accept. It just is.' I don't buy it. Her religious dedication is so...what's the word...banaal. I can't help that she can't think at a highaa level. She might even be delusional too. Well, it's a good thing she's not my problem anymore. I'm sure NOLAN can pray wit' 'er in New York.

"I wonder what Pergo would have thought about this stuff. He probably would have tried to put a positive spin on things. God, he was so naïve. Life nevaa comes out smellin' like cinnamon. My new therapist tells me that, 'We all want to be able to control the things that scare us. We're all looking for certainty. But the reality is that aging, sickness, and death can't be controlled. Thinking we are in control of anything is just a figment of our imagination. The only way to be healthy is to embrace the lack of control, accept the inevitabilities of existence, and live our lives with the freedom that accompanies it.' I think my therapist is delusional too. Well, maybe she's partly right. The damn uncertainty does plague us. I think it makes us all itch."

Epilogue

Pergo's Journal

[Entry 1] In life, the freedom to create is the highest calling. Yes, one can argue that writing is creative, but in my eyes, not to the same magnitude as painting. Painting is primitive. Painting shapes our reality; it can literally transform a person. Early peoples painted on cave walls. They told their stories with shapes and forms. Their stories told of human figures interacting with animals and spirits and nature. Life and death were captured in monochromatic shades. The truth in drawings was and is universal. It is simple. It is shared. Later generations look at these cave works and understand the intended messages. Art weaved a common thread fabricated across cultures and generations. This is not the same for the written word. The written word has far less utility. Even in one's native language, the written word requires translation. The written word lacks primal qualities. It is nuanced for some, and often spoken with insincere lips by others. Words are often deadened when they fall out of the mouths of the

educated—those who measure their thoughts like ingredients for a bread loaf. The written word is incapable of inspiring the same emotions as visual art. While writers try, they will always be held a distant second to painters in their intended effect. Zach was right all along.

[Entry 2] Complexity underscores how humans behave, or perhaps 'duplicity' is more appropriate. People make decisions from within. Information funnels through the senses as morning light enters east-facing windows.

In some cases, the beauty of the soothing ocean waves calms the essence of the house. The rhythm of the waves synchro-nizes your breathing. In and out, the cool smell of cloudy moisture tickles your nose and throat. Tranquility follows and there is peace in the house, peace within. Yet there are other times when the sunrise is covered by coastal storms; cyclones of water threaten the land, threaten the life, dissolve the peace. These instances make one seek comfort by turning the window shades down...to hide from the wrath. There is no doubt that the decision of what the world "is" is made on the inside (Clintonesque). The question is, should we open our shades or turn them?

In the east, the idea is to accept the sun and storms as the same. They are just slightly different colors of the rainbow of reality. One should appreciate the red, because without it, the blue does not resonate. The particles themselves—the photons, are as duplicitous as the light, masquerading as waves and then particles, or maybe neither. Some may realize that balance is found in the whole of things—not in the distinct and separate elements that comprise them.

[Entry 3] My wish—

The next day Chiara and her mom woke up early and took a ferryboat from Playa del Carmen to Cozumel. When they got there, they rented bicycles and rode a few miles to San Gervasio. *They walked around the ruins for an hour, and Chiara's mother explained that this was once a place where women would come to worship the goddess Ixchel. Chiara felt such an intense sense of wholeness being there with her mother. "I am so sorry for all that you have been through, Mom. I just want you to know that I love you, and I am just so happy to be able to be with you now."*

With a delicate kiss of her forehead, Chiara's mother said, "Those are the nicest words I've ever heard, Chiara. I love you too, with my entire being."

"Come on, let's get back over to the beach and go swimming. I'm hot."

They rode their bikes back to a secluded beach and rented some snorkeling equipment. They swam with the tropical fish and saw seahorses and turtles. The water cooled their heated bodies, broiled from the sun. They came out of the sea refreshed and rode their bikes back to the pier. There, they waited for their return ferry trip by drinking at Señor Frogs. They sipped margaritas from huge, orange plastic cups, danced with strangers, and split an order of soft tacos with green, spicy salsa. They giggled at the tourists wearing balloon hats and posing for photographs with the statue of the green frog. The fun lasted through the ferry ride back to the mainland. They were exhausted when they returned to the resort.

Later that night, when Chiara changed her clothes into something to sleep in, she asked her mom whether she would consider coming back to Boston with her to meet

Dan. Without pause, her mother rearranged her travel plans to accompany Chiara back to Beantown.

Chiara called Dan and told him the newest plan.

They were holding hands when they exited customs. Dan greeted them at the gate and Chiara ran into his arms and kissed him with the passion that grows with time and distance.

"There is someone I want you to meet, Dan. This is my mother."

"Very nice to meet you, ma'am. I am so glad to see you two had such a great trip together. It's great seeing you coming back whole."

Chiara's mother agreed and said, "Not as glad as I am, Dan. I want to cherish the gift that my daughter has given me, a second chance. It's also a pleasure to get to know the man she loves."

"Oh, thank you, ma'am. Nothing can destroy the energy between a mother and a daughter. I think that lives on in the paintings that Levy did of the two of you years back."

Chiara and her mother acknowledged the truth of his words.

With that, Dan grabbed both of their travel bags and drove them to his flat. They ate pizza and drank merlot while they discussed their favorite poets. Chiara's mom was not a fan of Dante. She thought he was too wordy.

Finally, when it was time for bed, Dan fixed his for the two of them and spent the night on the sofa. The next morning, he heard Chiara's mother wrestling around in the kitchen making breakfast. He could tell she was trying to walk quietly on his squeaky wooden floors. A few minutes later, he smelled the aroma of sugar and cinnamon.

They were finally home.

[Entry 4] The guilt eats at me like termites. I am sawdust, pencil shavings, dirt. Spirits distilled leave spirits unstill. Time cannot forgive that which is denied. Paths are personal, cheating is personal, justice is personal...death is personal. Eyes for eyes, I say with blurry vision. One can't rewrite life. Cast stones sink every time they hit the water...

[Entry 5] There are times when stories unfold and flood the senses, shutting them down with no further desire to feel. They look to me for answers, as if I can save them from themselves. If they only realized the emptiness of my vessel, and that we all need to descend into the barren circles alone. I am not their Virgil, and my Beatrice barely lives on with nothing but a pellucid look in her eyes. Her marred essence is a stain on my soul. Clarity is found under no lens. Words no longer abrogate sorrow. The California light shines no more, and even the lofty ideals of artful collages provide little solace. I will remain in the wood while dried branches are torn from my infested trunk.

Acknowledgements

I would like to thank Helene, Cheryl, Jenny, Paul, Tracy, Sarah, Maria, Michael, and Kyle for reviewing elements of this book.

About Atmosphere Press

Atmosphere Press is an independent, full-service publisher for excellent books in all genres and for all audiences. Learn more about what we do at atmospherepress.com.

We encourage you to check out some of Atmosphere's latest releases, which are available at Amazon.com and via order from your local bookstore:

Twisted Silver Spoons, a novel by Karen M. Wicks
Queen of Crows, a novel by S.L. Wilton
The Summer Festival is Murder, a novel by Jill M. Lyon
The Past We Step Into, stories by Richard Scharine
The Museum of an Extinct Race, a novel by Jonathan Hale Rosen
Swimming with the Angels, a novel by Colin Kersey
Island of Dead Gods, a novel by Verena Mahlow
Cloakers, a novel by Alexandra Lapointe
Twins Daze, a novel by Jerry Petersen
Embargo on Hope, a novel by Justin Doyle
Abaddon Illusion, a novel by Lindsey Bakken
Blackland: A Utopian Novel, by Richard A. Jones
The Jesus Nut, a novel by John Prather
The Embers of Tradition, a novel by Chukwudum Okeke
Saints and Martyrs: A Novel, by Aaron Roe
When I Am Ashes, a novel by Amber Rose
Melancholy Vision: A Revolution Series Novel, by L.C. Hamilton
The Recoleta Stories, by Bryon Esmond Butler
Voodoo Hideaway, a novel by Vance Cariaga

About the Author

Joseph Libonati holds his Ph.D. and is an award-winning professor. He has published numerous manuscripts in the discipline of cardiovascular physiology. He lives outside of Philadelphia, Pennsylvania.

Made in United States
North Haven, CT
04 February 2022

15669568R00150